T I M

MW01248457

MISSING

In Switzerland

TATE PUBLISHING
AND ENTERPRISES, LLC

Published by Tate Publishing & Enterprises, LLC
127 E. Trade Center Terrace | Mustang, Oklahoma 73064 USA
1.888.361.9473 | www.tatepublishing.com

Tate Publishing is committed to excellence in the publishing industry. The company reflects the philosophy established by the founders, based on Psalm 68:11,
"The Lord gave the word and great was the company of those who published it."

Book design copyright © 2015 by Tate Publishing, LLC. All rights reserved.
Cover design by Samson Lim
Interior design by Jomar Ouano

Published in the United States of America

ISBN: 978-1-68187-231-5
1. Fiction / Action & Adventure
2. Fiction / Mystery & Detective / Private Investigators
15.08.26

1

I was worn down to a frazzle when I quit the Quaboag Metropolitan Police Force after twenty long years of getting shot at, spit on by druggies with AIDS, and having my suits ripped to shreds by the pit bulls the dealers used to protect their stash. Who knew if there were infected needles in the pockets of the homeless bums I had rounded up when I frisked them for weapons? The risk sure wasn't worth the pittance being direct deposited into my checking account. At least when I was in the service, I got a combat pay bonus to help compensate for hazardous duty in the war zones.

The constant vigilance and sleepless nights had taken its toll not only on me, but almost more so, on my lovely, former wife. Melanie walked out on me twelve years ago. She could no longer take raising the kids as if she were a single parent with me acting as if I was a boat anchor, pulling her down into the cesspool that I called work. Maybe if I had not called to cancel going to the meetings at school with Ryan and Jesse at the last minute so many times. Perhaps I could have explained to Captain Norris how important it was for me to show up for dinner before it was ruined, even once in a while.

That was then. This is now. I have done fairly well as a private detective over the past five years. The work was a natural extension of what I had done in the military and on the police force, except I no longer had to follow somebody else's rules. For me, the assignments were easy. I liked being my own boss and enjoyed the work more without being told how, when, and what to do. That's with the caveat that I can keep finding enough clients to stay busy and earn a living.

In most jobs I have taken on, I had to locate a missing person or follow a spouse to see if they were cheating. With today's electronics, a magnetic GPS bug placed under a car made tailing a suspect at a safe distance a snap. Intercepting cell phones with variable frequency scanners makes one wonder why people who want privacy would go the wireless route. Parabolic listening devices permit eavesdropping on conversations across the street from a distance of up to a hundred yards away.

The electronic "paper trail" left by credit and debit cards makes it extremely difficult for anyone to hide. Information available to the public on the Internet via Google and the credit reporting agencies on just about everyone is there for the taking if you know where to look. It's a good thing I took those computer courses in night school when I left the police force.

Life has been good since then, except it has usually been feast or famine as far as cases go. Three weeks ago, I had located a runaway teen. Traci's parents were so grateful to have her back home safe and sound they threw in an extra five grand as a bonus. She probably won't run away again because she appeared to have learned her lesson.

I found Traci holed up in a fleabag hotel down in Queens after her boyfriend had abandoned her. He said he was going to find a job and come back for her. He didn't even try to call her after he left. She had run out of money and was getting desperate when I found her. At age fourteen, they were too young to get married without parental permission and had no luck finding work. It seems that even the employers with menial jobs would rather take a reliable illegal alien who couldn't speak English than kids who were perpetually late or didn't show up at all. For fear of being deported, the illegals would also work for less than minimum wage without complaining so they wouldn't be reported to the INS.

Since then *nada*, *zilch*! I was listed with a block ad in the Yellow Pages as "Powers Investigations." I also had a website that a nephew had put together for me with eye-catching graphics. They both were professional looking, and I did get a fair number of referrals from most of the major search engines. Unfortunately, as far as business is concerned, I had hit the doldrums lately with nary a trade wind blowing. It is hard to plan your next move when your business is dead in the water.

As I was thinking there must be something positive I could do to find more cases instead of just glancing at the phone and willing it to ring, there was a gentle knock at the door. I swiveled in my chair and looked up at the frosted glass window. Beyond the reverse image of *Powers Investigations*, I could clearly see the outline of a woman.

Leaning forward to open the door, I was taken aback by the vision of an exceptionally attractive woman before me looking angelic with her windblown hair covered with a light dusting of snow. I'm six feet, two inches, but I was surprised that she was almost as tall as I was. She had to be at least five foot, ten or eleven without the stiletto heels. Her large brown eyes looked as soft and gentle as those of a deer. She didn't flinch in response to my staring and maintained full eye contact.

When I recovered my composure and closed my mouth, I said, "Please come in."

She asked, "Are you Mr. Thomas Powers?"

My office was located over a furniture store in a remodeled brick building of former Victorian elegance in the heart of downtown Quaboag. She was still breathy from climbing the stairs and reminded me of Marilyn Monroe in her old movies shown on late-night TV. "Yes, I am. How may I help you?" I replied as I walked around the desk to sit down, my voice dropping an octave.

Entering my office, she removed her scarf and long overcoat and then hung them on the coat rack in the corner. "My name is Monique Pickering," she said in a troubled yet melodious tone. "My husband Peter has disappeared, and the police in Europe have been unable to help. Some close friends told me that you are very good at what you do."

Because she was so well endowed, I couldn't help but think of the old Vaudeville shtick that went, "A lady walked into my office and pointed a pair of 38s at me. Then she drew a gun." That's when I told myself I've got to stop watching those old movies on late-night television.

Forcing myself to focus back on the current moment, she was perfectly proportioned. The short skirt and plunging neckline that exposed so much skin on a cold day suggested she could be a blond bimbo, however. This contradicted the expensive clothing and perfume she wore. Either she was an exhibitionist or just very comfortable with herself and didn't care what anyone else thought.

I said, "Please have a seat and tell me what you know about your husband's disappearance so far," as I gestured toward a client chair that faced the oversized mahogany desk.

She sat down gracefully and crossed her very shapely legs. It seemed I was bothered more than she was by her abbreviated skirt being hiked up well past the point that decency should have allowed.

Now that she had fully recovered from the climb up the long flight of stairs, I detected a hint of a French accent, but with perfect upper crust English diction. The social circles she traveled in probably accounted for the avant-garde fashion statement she was making or made without caring one way or another.

"Please start at the beginning. When and where did he disappear?" I asked as I studied her facial expressions for clues.

"Peter was on a business trip in Zurich, Switzerland. He was to meet me two weeks ago at the Waldorf Astoria Hotel in Amsterdam after I visited with my family in France, but he never showed up," she said, wiping a tear from her cheek with the back of her hand, her voice cracking.

"What did you do then?" I asked, nudging a box of tissues across the desk in her direction.

Reaching for a Kleenex and stifling a sob, she replied, "I contacted Interpol and the Swiss Police. They could find no trace of him after he checked out of the Widder Hotel. He never boarded his KLM flight at the airport."

"Did you check anywhere else?" I asked.

"The American Embassy said they would post an internal bulletin at all their European locations. Then they suggested I fly home to the States in case he tries to contact me here," she said, somehow managing arrest the quiver in her voice.

At first I wondered for a nanosecond if Monique might want to find the body to collect on an insurance policy, but then I could tell from the hesitations in her speech and general demeanor just how distraught she really was.

I asked, "Did Peter Pickering have any enemies?"

She said, "No. Everyone who knew Peter really liked him. His ability to make anyone he dealt with feel important won him many lifelong friends. He was that kind of person. He has been my best friend almost since the day we first met at his London office eleven years ago. I was just starting out in sales for the French company Choquette Industrielles."

"What do they do, and where are they located?" I asked.

"They are a nameplate and membrane switch manufacturer near the Rhine in the northeast of France in the village of Marckolsheim. It didn't seem to matter that we were one of Peter's smaller vendors, he devoted the same attention and courtesies to us as he did to his major suppliers," she replied.

Her whole persona seemed to change when talking about her husband. It was as if she were surrounded by the warm glow of his protective aura. A smile fleetingly crossed her lips and her voice grew steadier, looking down at something that only she could see. Not that she appeared to need any protection. Her poise suggested she could handle herself quite well in any situation.

"What kind of business was he involved in?" I asked.

Monique paused and then said, "Import and export of components for durable consumer goods."

"What kind of durable goods?" I asked.

Monique said, "Everything from automobiles, appliances, tools, business machines, computers and communications equipment to electronics."

"Do any of his business associates or competitors have an axe to grind with Peter?"

"No. I have met many of them at international trade shows and meetings. They only have good things to say about Peter in private," Monique answered.

"Have you ever witnessed anything in his business dealings or travel that seemed to be a little bit peculiar or out of the ordinary?" I asked, trying to take notes fast enough to keep up with the conversation and not miss pertinent facts.

Reflecting a moment, she said, "The one thing that might have made me suspicious from time to time was his seemingly unplanned meetings with men who appeared to be overdressed in suits and ties on casual occasions. It was always in strange, out-of-the-way places when we were traveling.

"Peter is normally quite open with me about everything and introduces me to all of his business acquaintances. When I asked about these men, he sloughed it off and became uncharacteristically evasive. I once suggested they look like they could be government employees. That was when Peter appeared to be very uncomfortable and became quiet. After that, I never mentioned them again."

"I have to ask, has Peter ever received any threats?"

Apparently surprised that she didn't remember to mentioned it sooner, she said, "Oh! I have been so worried and upset by all this, I almost forgot this came in the mail today."

She reached into her purse and produced a folded envelope addressed to their home in the neighboring town of Westmoreland, Massachusetts. She gingerly handled it by the edges to preserve any evidence of fingerprints. I tried my best to ignore the sight of her barely restrained breasts as she leaned forward to pass the envelope to me over the desk.

From the slope and unevenness of the writing on the envelope, it appeared that a right hander printed it in block letters with his or her left hand. Inside on the note were small letters and words clipped from magazines and pasted on a page that read,

"STOP LOOKING FOR YOUR HUSBAND
OR
YOU WILL BE NEXT."

"Have you or Peter had any other threats before this or unusual phone calls?" I asked.

Monique thought for a minute and replied, "There have been some mysterious phone calls during the night in the past. When there were no answers on the other end, I would dismiss them as wrong numbers."

"Do you have a recent picture of Peter?" I inquired.

"Yes, here in this folder," she said as a she handed it to me. "I included a list of contacts for our jointly owned business offices here and overseas. I also wrote down the details of my dealings with the American Embassy in Bern, Interpol, and the Swiss officials since Peter disappeared. I hope all this will help."

"Yes, I'm sure it will be extremely useful, thank you," I said.

Although we had not discussed my billing rate, I noticed a cashier's check for fifty thousand US dollars was enclosed as a retainer. Surprised, I said, "You didn't even ask about my fee. You should know my standard rate is one thousand dollars a day plus expenses. I'll need to have you sign this contract to make it legal," I added as I filled in the blanks.

"If you can find Peter, whatever you charge will be worth it. Thank you very much in advance for your time and prompt attention to this matter, Mr. Powers," she said. "I feel much better already knowing that you will be actively searching for Peter. The people on the Continent were polite but seemed to be just going through the motions."

"Please call me Tom. Mr. Powers is my dad. Would you mind if I call you Monique?"

"You Americans are always on a first-name business. No, I do not mind at all. That is what my friends here in the States call me, but if you will excuse me, I would like to return home as soon as possible in case Peter tries to reach me."

"Apparently you've been very thorough, but please contact me if you think of anything else. Even something that appears to be insignificant could be the missing piece to the puzzle we're trying to solve," I said as I handed her my business card.

Then I asked, "Do you have anyone to stay with you?"

"No, but the housekeeper will come early tomorrow morning for the weekly cleaning of our chateau in the Berkshires," she said.

"Since we don't know who we're dealing with, I'll have my cousin Janyce come over to spend the night. She is a part-time police officer in Westmoreland. Janyce will make three quick raps on the door and show her badge when she gets there. Don't open the door to anyone else," I told her as I walked around the desk to help her on with her coat.

2

After calling my former partner in the Quaboag Municipal Police Department, I followed up by sending Monique's envelope and letter by messenger to be checked for fingerprints and DNA traces. Jerry said he'd sneak them into the schedule and put a rush on the tests.

With the differences in European time zones of either five or six hours from here, I first phoned the American embassies in Bern, Switzerland, and The Hague, Netherlands, before the regular staffers left for the weekend. Then I called the police and the Missing Persons Bureau in Zurich, Switzerland next. They had no news to report since Monique had asked them for help.

Interpol was manned around the clock as well, so I followed up those contacts with a Captain Vito Annitti. He spoke in broken English, but his English was much better than the few words of Italian I had acquired dealing with Mafia informants over the years.

It turned out they had located a John Doe in the Stuttgart General Hospital Trauma Ward in Germany who fit the general description of Peter Pickering. When he finally woke from his coma, he had no idea who he was or how he got there. Because the back of his head had been bashed in, they ran an MRI and determined that he had sustained a substantial concussion. Interpol could find no match of his fingerprints or DNA in their databases.

Vito was working from a small wallet-sized photo that was significantly older than the recent one Monique had just given me. I scanned the new photo into my computer and e-mailed it to Captain Annitti at Interpol for distribution.

Then I dialed Monique at her home. She picked up after four rings and sounded out of breath again. I said, "Hi, Monique. It's Tom Powers."

"Hello, Tom. I am glad I caught you in time. I just pulled into the driveway and had the key in the lock when the phone rang. It took longer than I expected to get home with all the snow coming down."

"I don't want to get your hopes up, but it's possible I may have a lead," I told her. "There's a man in a Stuttgart hospital in Germany without any documentation that fits Peter's general description, but he has a case of complete amnesia. His face is swollen and bandaged up so they can't compare him to Peter's photo. It's probably a long shot since we don't know how Peter could have ended up in Germany from Switzerland. Do you know who Peter's dentist is?"

Monique said, "He mostly went to a Dr. Robert Sullivan in Framingham. Sullivan's location was convenient to Peter's main office for the Three P Company here in the States, but that was before we moved out here to the Berkshires to get away from the noise and traffic."

"I'll arrange to have his dental records compared to the patient in Germany, just on the outside chance that it could be him," I said.

"Please let me know as soon as you hear anything back," she said. "Oh! There's a woman getting out of a red Jeep that just pulled up in the drive. Is your cousin a tall brunette? Never mind. She rapped three times on the door, and she's holding up her badge to the monitor. It must be her. I will talk to you later. Good-bye for now."

I checked my computer. I had an e-mail from a Sergeant Wolfgang Hollock of the Stuttgart Police in Germany. A detailed description of Peter had been received from Interpol along with the new photograph, but there was still too much swelling and abrasions on the face of the John Doe to draw a conclusion. At the request of Captain Annitti at Interpol, Hollock had sent copies of the John Doe's prints and DNA scan to me. I thanked Sergeant Hollock for the information and replied that I would have Dr. Sullivan send a copy of the digitalized dental X-rays directly to him in Stuttgart at the same time he sends them to me.

It was almost 3:30 PM, EST, when I dialed information to obtain the number of the dentist in Framingham. I called him immediately, but Dr. Sullivan said he uses MedStore, Inc. in Natick as an outside retrieval service for digital conversion and computer storage of his X-rays. Unfortunately, he said they closed for the weekend at 3:00 PM. He promised he'd follow up with them when they reopen on Monday and get back to me.

I decided to ring up an old school chum who was in charge of spooky stuff over the pond at the state department. I was greeted with a very pleasant-sounding voice who said, "Good afternoon, International Affairs. How may I direct your call?"

"Hello, Mr. Alexander Wisniewski, please," I said, surprised that a woman that cheerful could work for our federal government.

"He's in conference at the moment," said the voice with a smile in it. "Will he know what this is regarding?"

"No, he won't. Just tell him it's Scooter on the line," I said with a grin, remembering what he looked like when we were kids together and he was known in the neighborhood as Boomer.

In a few minutes, he was on the phone. "Tom! It's been a long time. How are Melanie and the kids?"

"Hi, Alex, it's great to hear your voice again, but Melanie left with the kids a dozen years ago. She could no longer tolerate me putting the job ahead of her and the family anymore. Ryan is a senior at MIT and Jesse is a sophomore at Brown University. You're absolutely right, though. It has been far too long. Is this a good time?"

"The meeting I was in dragged on for hours, and I needed a break anyway. I was just in the middle of being transferred from the European Operations to head up our Mid-East Branch so everything is in transition. I'll be glad when things settle down again. What's up, Tom?"

"Sounds like congratulations are in order," I said.

"Not really, Tom. It's more of a lateral move. We've got sufficient staff in Europe to maintain status quo, but the previous Mediterranean director was blown up in Baghdad by an Iranian-supplied IED last week. I just happen to have prior experience working with the Arabs in several countries."

"Never knew you were an alpha male of the organization. I'm impressed, Alex, but keep your head down. The reason I called is that I need to ask a big favor of you."

"Just name it, old friend."

"Well, Alex, about five years ago, I took early retirement from the police and started all over again as a private Dick. I have a client whose husband disappeared without a trace on a business trip to Europe a couple of weeks ago. He checked out of his hotel but never made it to his flight from Zurich, Switzerland, to Amsterdam. No one has seen him since.

A John Doe with amnesia turned up with his approximate description in Germany, but the authorities in Europe couldn't match his fingerprints or DNA with their records.

Since you're into cloak-and-dagger operations, I thought you might be able to check them against the military and civilian government files."

"Tell you what, Tom, when we say good-bye, stay on the phone and my administrative assistant will get your Internet address and phone numbers. Then she can follow up with an e-mail to you. When you receive it, just send the prints and DNA chart as attachments and hit 'Reply.' Don't even put a subject. It will already be encrypted to clear security."

"*Wow!* That's even slicker than the magic spy decoders we used as kids," I said. "How's life been treating you by the way? Are you still a confirmed bachelor, Alex?"

"I met a woman in negotiations with several former Soviet satellite countries some time back. She works in the next building here and understands the demands of my position, so it's a great fit. Carla's sharp as a tack and a wonderful cook. We moved in together about three years ago," he said.

"Sounds like you're living at the top of the heap. Can't wait to meet her the next time I'm in Washington. I really appreciate your help on this one. I'll owe you big time. Just let me know when I can reciprocate. Take care of yourself, Alex," I said.

"You do the same, Tom. Stay on the phone to give Sue your particulars."

3

After I hung up the phone, I immediately sent the information to Alex. It was then I realized I'd forgotten about eating lunch, so I headed across the street to the American House on Main Street. The restaurant was on the first floor of an old hotel. It was quaint with all the original gas light fixtures converted to electric, dark walnut moldings and decorative tin ceiling tiles. A young couple had bought the place and seemed to be more interested in making friends than profits.

"Hi, Sally, I'll have a corn beef on rye and a cup of the best coffee in the city."

"Hi, Tom, you look a little tired. Maybe this will pick you up." Sally had anticipated the coffee request and was pouring before she left to place the order with her husband Gary in the kitchen.

Sally brought out a sandwich that had to be held together with a long toothpick because it was at least two inches thick between the oversized slices of home baked bread. There was hardly room for the big dill pickle and all the French fries on the large oval platter.

Before I finished eating, Sally refilled the coffee mug and put a piece of hot apple pie I hadn't ordered next to my dinner plate. "It's fresh from the oven. Gary thought you might like a piece."

"That's not fair, you know I can't resist. They're gonna have to carry me out of here," I told her.

I headed home to my apartment feeling totally overstuffed. I was thinking that if they don't stop treating me like family at the American House, I'll have to find a place to eat with smaller portions and less-appetizing food.

As I was walking in from the car, the ring on my cell phone jerked me back to reality. It was Alex. He said they had obtained a fingerprint identification of the John Doe. Turns out he was an operative for the CIA in the civilian files under a code name. The American Embassy staff in Berlin had already sent a medical and security team on their way to pick him up and transport him back to the States in a military Medevac plane.

Alex said, "This is the guy you were looking for. There are e-tickets at the Albany airport booked for you in your name as Mr. and Mrs. You will be waved through security. Pick up your client and take Delta flight 2411 out of Albany, NY, at

10:00 PM tonight to Washington-Dulles Airport in DC. I will meet you at the gate when you land."

"Boy, talk about fast service. What can I tell my client?" I asked.

"Only tell her the minimum you can get away with. Her husband is recovering physically but still has a severe case of amnesia. Hopefully it's temporary. See you soon. Good-bye," he said abruptly.

I called the Pickering house and Janyce answered. "Hi, Janyce, it will be a shorter night for you after all. Tell Monique to pack a bag for two or three days away as fast as she can. I'll explain when I get there. If she needs anything else, she can buy it when we arrive at our destination. The snow isn't letting up, so I'll need you to take us to the Albany airport with your four-wheel-drive Jeep."

"You're being kind of mysterious Tom," Janyce said.

"Fill you in later, kid. Bye for now," I said.

Fortunately, the snowplows had cleared Route 7 from Quaboag down to Westmoreland. My front wheel drive with all weather tires may be okay to get to the airport, but why take a chance in this stuff?

The women had warmed up the Jeep and were ready to go when I got there. Janyce looked surprised when I sat in the backseat with Monique instead of up front. "Janyce, take Route I-90 out to the Albany airport as fast as you can comfortably drive in this storm. It wouldn't hurt if you were to use the flashing police lights."

"You're the boss, Tom, but the law says I have to shut them off when I cross the state line," Janyce replied while turning on her roof-mounted lights.

Naturally Monique seemed to be thoroughly confused at this point. I turned to her and said, "I've got good news and bad news. The man I told you about who was in a coma at the hospital in Germany turned out to be Peter. As we speak, he's being flown to the Washington, DC, beltway. We're on our way to meet him there. The bad news is that he sustained a severe concussion and has total amnesia. It may be only temporary, but they don't know yet."

"I do not understand. Why would they fly him to Washington?" Monique asked.

One could tell how worried Monique was just by looking at her. It seemed that her whole life revolved around Peter.

"An old friend of mine says Peter had been doing clandestine work for the US Department of State," I said. "The people you told me about Peter meeting secretly on your trips together may have been government officials from the United States. The work he was doing for them could explain why he was attacked in Switzerland," I said. "They flew him to the Walter Reed National Military Medical Center to make certain he had the best care available."

Janice handled the Jeep through the snow like a pro and drove us right up the departure ramp at the terminal. I took the luggage and thanked her. Janyce closed up the back of the Jeep and turned to give me a big hug. Monique and I were ushered through security and seated immediately as the door closed. The plane took off down the runway and we were up in the air in short order. We barely made the flight—talk about good timing.

4

Alex was waiting next to a limo with a pair of black SUV security escorts on the tarmac when we taxied to the gate. I'm sure the rest of the passengers on the flight wondered who were the dignitaries being greeted at the base of the ramp. We were then ushered to the procession of cars parked on the runway.

Alex walked over, shook my hand, and gave me a big bear hug as soon as I stepped off the stairs. "Tom, great to see you again old buddy."

"Hi, Alex, same here," I said, stepping back giving him the once over. "You're looking well."

Turning to Monique, I said, "I'd like to introduce Alexander Wisniewski of the US Department of State. Alex, this is Monique Pickering."

Following introductions, Alex led us to the limo, and we were whisked away into the night in the caravan of three black government vehicles with tinted windshields. It seemed odd that all the traffic lights were green in our favor at every intersection until I realized the SUV in front of us had to be clearing the way with a remote radio frequency controller.

Alex explained to Monique that Peter had been asked by the United States government to help identify agents in China, North Korea, Pakistan, and Iran who ordered certain components from the United States that could be used to advance their rocket and missile programs.

"We think they are the ones who hit him over the head and left him for dead in Germany. We are making sure he's getting the proper treatment to speed his recovery. A team of top neurologists are being flown in to consult on his condition."

The mini-caravan pulled up to the new Walter Reed Medical Complex in Bethesda, Maryland. We were then directed to an executive conference room paneled with what appeared to be hand-rubbed oak framed with elaborate trim.

A large breakfast of eggs, sausage, bacon, toast, and pancakes was brought in with steaming hot coffee as Monique and I filled out form after form for security clearances.

Upon issuance of temporary badges, we were brought up to a secure level, accessible only with a special elevator key. Arriving at the floor, we found armed guards were posted on both sides of the car doors and at the entrance to the private room at the other end of the hall.

Alex flashed his credentials on the way through the door as Monique all but ran toward Peter's bedside. She stopped short in the doorway when she saw his head was wrapped up like an Indian sheik's turban. He resembled an exploding can of Chef Boyardee pasta with all the tubes and wires emanating from him.

"Peter, Peter!" she exclaimed, before she backed off, afraid to touch him lest she hit a tender spot. "Can you hear me?"

A tall, lean, dark-skinned doctor with penetrating eyes was standing on the opposite side of the bed. He glanced at her identification badge and said, "I am very sorry, Mrs. Pickering, but aside from an occasional twitch, I'm afraid your husband has been totally unresponsive since being put into a chemically induced coma upon his arrival. We had to operate to relieve the pressure building up inside his skull.

"I'm Dr. Saad, chief of Neurology. We are hoping that he will start to regain his memory once the inflammation in his brain subsides. We want to allow him time to come out of the coma naturally. Until that happens, we will try to let him recover from the rest of his injuries at his own pace."

Not certain what that meant, Monique blurted out, "Do…do you know how long that m-might take?"

The doctor replied, "We believe the internal swelling will diminish sufficiently in the next week or two that we will be able to slowly wean him off the conscious suppression drugs. Then it will be up to his body to determine when he will awaken. It could be another week, or it could take as long as a month."

"Would it be okay for me to stay with him?" Monique almost pleaded.

"We can arrange to have a cot brought in for you. The nurse's name is Lisa Ransom. She will get you whatever else you need," the doctor said.

Alex turned to the doctor while writing on his business card, shook his hand, and said, "Thank you for everything, Dr. Saad. Here is my card. My cell phone number is written on the back. Please keep me posted on Peter's progress and feel free to contact me if there is anything I can expedite for you."

"Mrs. Pickering, Dr. Saad is one of the top neurosurgeons in the world. Peter will be getting the best of care. There are things I have to discuss with Tom. We'll be back to check on you later," Alex said as he turned to leave.

Monique immediately threw her arms around Alex, almost bowling him over as she said, "Thank you, thank you so much for everything you have done."

Alex looked surprised as he untangled himself from Monique before she turned to me and proceeded to give me the same treatment plus a kiss on the cheek. "Tom, I do not know how I can ever thank you for finding Peter so fast. I was almost beginning to give up hope," Monique said, shuttering with a sigh of relief.

I told her, "You need to try to relax. Alex arranged for all of this to happen. You're in good hands. Dr. Saad will look after Peter's recovery, and Alex will see to your safety. I'll be back in a little while."

I followed Alex back down the corridor to the elevator. When the car arrived, he got in and pushed the button for the third floor. As soon as we were out of earshot from the guards at the door, Alex turned to me and said, "Wow, Monique certainly is demonstrative, isn't she?"

"We just met this week, so it's kind of hard for me to judge. I could tell she was extremely anxious on the trip down here, but I suspect she was so worried about her husband she didn't know what to say," I replied.

When the elevator door opened, Alex led the way down the hall to a smaller conference room than the one we were in before. "Have a seat, Tom. Would you like a cup of coffee?" he asked.

"I thought you'd never ask. It's been a while since I've pulled an all-nighter," I said.

Alex grabbed the pot and a couple of mugs from the credenza against the wall. Pouring two cups, he said, "Tom, I've talked to the powers that be in the State Department. They have agreed to reinstate the same level of security clearance you had when you worked for the Army Military Intelligence Corps so we can discuss Peter Pickering's situation in full detail. Since you are already involved in this case, I've been authorized to offer you a consulting position at your standard billing rate if you're still interested when we finish our discussion here."

"It so happens that I have time available at the moment," I said. "What can you tell me about what an English businessman was doing working undercover for the United States Central Intelligence Agency?"

"Well, Tom, I'm sure you are aware that the government regulates and restricts the transfer and export of information, commodities and technology deemed strategically important to the security of the United States," Alex said. "We are especially concerned with preventing countries that sponsor terrorists from getting their hands on American technology and using it against us."

"I'm sure we could do a better job of enforcing our laws and regulations, but what does that have to do with Peter?" I asked.

"Peter is more involved with supplying industry with what you might call old-school technology for things like controls and switches. The electro-mechanical devices are more like analogue televisions than digital ones," Alex explained.

"So why would these countries want the old-school technology, as you put it?" I asked, confused.

"While we try to prevent certain countries from obtaining our latest technology and components with advanced mechanisms, we have not exercised due diligence in keeping finished product assemblies of durable goods that contain them from being sold indiscriminately on the open market. They simply purchase cars, appliances, and equipment to remove the computer controls and upgraded subassemblies," Alex said.

"What does that buy them?" I asked.

"They do not have to try to set up sophisticated, precision manufacturing to make them. These new technology controls and sensors can be incorporated directly into their missiles, rockets, and weapons at a fraction of the cost our government pays for them from our military and aerospace firms," Alex said.

"Oh, I get it. They replace the high-tech stuff in the finished products they purchased with the old-fashioned controls, bells, and whistles so the units can still be resold," I said. "You're telling me, Peter was trying to keeping track of which countries were removing our state-of-the-art widgets and replacing them with the obsolete toggle switches and electro-mechanical controls."

"Yep, it took a while for us to figure out what they were doing with all the analogue parts. We didn't know they were using our technologies in their weapon systems until a number of pieces were captured. Tracing back the serial numbers of the components, we found out where they came from," Alex said.

"And Peter was providing you with his customer lists?" I asked.

"Yeah, that was one way we thought we could keep track of the countries that were busy making weapons of mass destruction and supplying the terrorists with them. Unfortunately, they were being ordered by trading companies and reshipped, so we had trouble determining the final destinations. We also have been trying to identify the Chinese nationals who were taking computer controls destined for US appliances and adapting them to use in ICBMs for possible sale to places like Iran and Nigeria," Alex replied.

"Do you have any idea who found out Peter was working with the CIA?" I asked.

"Not as yet," Alex said. "We assume that they left him for dead when they dumped him in Germany. Hopefully they are no longer looking for him, and maybe they'll leave his wife alone. That's why no one can know that he's still alive."

"I already cautioned Monique not to tell anyone where she is or say anything about Peter. We should get word out to the American Embassies in Europe to quietly call off the search for him," I said.

"I'll take care of that," Alex said. "There is one thing you can help us on first. Peter took meticulous notes on his business transactions for us. We haven't seen the latest entries, so finding his record book would be extremely helpful."

"I'll talk to Monique about it. Maybe he kept it at home or in his office here," I said.

"Now that you know the details, is this something you want to be involved with again, Tom?" Alex asked. "You already know the rest of the drill and what's required."

"I guess you can consider me on the clock, or will be as soon as I can get a few hours sleep," I said.

As Alex extended his hand, he said, "Welcome aboard then. I'll see what I can do about finding you an empty hospital bed here for now."

5

"Huh, what, where am I? Oh, it's you Alex. What's going on?" I asked.

"It's late afternoon, Tom. I brought you a lunch tray I snagged from the cafeteria," Alex said. "You were snoring so peacefully, I hated to wake you, but I figured you'd want to get going. That way the rest of the people on this floor can take a nap."

"Hey, Boomer, you know I don't snore that loud, but thank you for the tray anyway. Let me see if I can figure out which end is up. It tastes like a camel walked out of the desert and over my tongue. At least the coffee doesn't smell institutional," I said, inhaling deeply. "Mmm, the coffee tastes as great as it smells. Much better than what they served at officers' mess in the army. Thank you."

Alex stepped to one side and said, "While you are becoming coherent eating that sandwich, I'd like to introduce you to Joan Walters, formerly a lieutenant in Army Military Intelligence. She has been involved on the case from the beginning, processing the data obtained from Mr. Pickering on prior reports. She will be working with you to help gather information in the field. Joan, this is Tom Powers, private detective and all around good guy."

Moving the tray table aside and standing to shake hands, I said to the exceptionally attractive young woman, "I'm very pleased to meet you, Ms. Walters. I will need to talk to you at length to obtain your input, but I do a solo act. I'm afraid I can't do my job and be responsible for your safety at the same time."

Rising to his full height, Alex turned to me and glared as he said, "Tom, I wouldn't have obtained her services to work with you if I didn't think it was absolutely necessary and potentially beneficial.

"For your information, she is qualified as an expert marksman and has a black belt in karate. She can take care of herself and watch your back. There may be some element of danger associated with this assignment. Peter was attacked and his wife already received a threatening letter."

"Okay, okay. We'll give it a try and see how it works out," I said, wondering if someone that gorgeous can be bright enough to be useful as well.

After a short pause, Walters looked at me, offered her hand with a smile, and said, "Hopefully we can work together and help each other out along the way. To clear the air, let's start fresh, Mr. Powers. It'll probably be easier if you just call me Joan."

"Only if you call me Tom," I said with a meek grin after my outburst while I shook her hand.

"Now that's settled, perhaps we can go up to see how the Pickerings are doing," Alex said, leading the way out of the room without waiting for a response.

The guards were still stationed at both ends of the corridor as we walked down the hall and entered the patient's room. Monique was engrossed in reading a book to Peter. She stopped, looked up, and said, "I have heard that people in a coma can sometimes hear what is going on, even if they are unable to respond."

Alex asked, "Has there been any change in his condition?"

"None, other than an occasional involuntary movement. The doctor said not to expect any real progress for at least a week or two. He said that if Peter hears a familiar voice, it certainly would not hurt in speeding up his recovery," Monique replied.

"Mrs. Pickering, this is Joan Walters. She will be working with Tom to find out who attacked Peter and help round them up."

Reaching out, she said, "I suspect we'll be seeing each other from time to time, so please call me Joan."

"In that case, you may call me Monique," she said while shaking hands.

I said, "Monique, I understand Peter kept a journal on his business transactions. Do you know where it would be? It might help to take a look at his latest contacts."

"It could be at home in his desk in the den or in his Framingham office. We have not started to move our business to our new location in the Berkshires as yet," she said. "I will provide the panel punch codes for the gate and the house security system next to the front door. This is the house key. You may remove it from the ring while I write down the codes for you. The Boston line for our Massachusetts business office is (617) 711-3000. Ask for Lucille. I will inform her that you will be in touch soon."

"Thank you, Monique," I said as I wrote the number down. "As usual, you have been very thorough. Please make sure you don't tell her or anyone else where you are or that you know where Peter is. You both will be safer if whoever attacked Peter doesn't know he survived."

Alex said, "There's a snowstorm blowing through the Albany area, Tom, so I'll have them book you and Joan on the 5:00 PM Jet Blue flight this afternoon to Boston Logan so you can start looking for Peter's journal in the Three P Company office. I happen to have taken that flight last week. The e-ticket reservations will be available at the Jet Blue airport ticket counter."

"That's great, Alex. While we're there, I'm sure it won't hurt to talk to the staff at the Framingham office to see what we can learn about Peter's arrangements for his most recent trip to Europe and who he was planning to meet," I said.

"Joan, do you have a bag packed?" Alex asked.

"Always," Joan answered simply.

Monique turned to me with the list of security codes in hand and said, "I will call Lucille right away so she will be expecting you. She should be able to answer all of your questions."

"Joan and I will do our best to find out who did this to Peter," I said. "Alex will make certain that you and Peter will be taken care of while we're away."

Monique wrapped her arms around me again and with tears streaming down her cheeks said, "Thank you so much, Tom. I do not know what I would have done without your help."

"It's all part of the service. We'll do everything we can to round up the bad guys. Good-bye for now," I said.

On the way back down the hallway, I grabbed my suitcase from my temporary quarters.

Alex walked us back to the elevator and said, "Joan has been on assignment to our department because of overlap with prior cases with which she was involved. She will have dotted line responsibility to you, but since she grew up in the Boston area and has street savvy, you may want to defer to her judgment on some issues."

Turning to Joan, Alex looked her in the eye and said, "I wouldn't have taken Tom on if he wasn't good, so you can listen to what he says too. I know you both have excellent track records and are confident when working on your own. If you function as a team, I feel there could be exceptional synergy if you both try hard to make it come together and learn to depend on one another. Good luck to you both."

We shook hands with Alex at the elevator door. He said, "Contact me if there's anything you need. It was great to see you again, Tom."

The doors closed, and Joan started to say something to me when her cell phone rang. Holding up her index finger, she said, "Oh, hi, Dad. Now's not a good time to talk. I'm just leaving on a trip out of town. I'll call you as soon as I can."

Pausing for a reply, she said, "No, Dad, I'm not traveling alone, so don't worry."

With an exasperated look on her face, she waited for her father to complete his response and then said, "We've been through all this before. If you must know he was an officer in the military and a former police detective, so I'll be well protected. I've got to go now."

After another long pause, she said, "Yes, he is, but it doesn't matter, because that's not going to happen."

Rolling her eyes, Joan tried impatiently to break back into the conversation, "Dad…Dad, I really have to go. Love you. I'll be in touch soon," she said then hung up her phone.

The elevator doors opened. Joan looked up at me and said, "I'm sorry you had to listen to all that. According to him, I'm still his little girl. He also lives in the past and wanted to remind me for the zillionth time how difficult mixed marriages can be."

"Isn't he getting ahead of himself? Does he have a problem with different religions? You don't know what faith I practice, and you're not that much older than my daughter," I said, confused.

"No, that's not it," she replied. He goes through the same scenario every time I work with a white guy."

"Oh, he's one of those," I said. "He has nothing to be concerned with on that score. I've never dated co-workers and don't plan to start now."

Joan said, "My car is over in the visitors' lot. I often don't know in advance when I'll go on my next trip, so I keep a packed bag in the trunk."

After I followed her out to her car, she popped the trunk lid of her bright red Shelby Cobra. I threw my bag in with hers and closed it. I was able to reach in to move the passenger seat all the way back, but after sitting my butt on the seat, it was difficult to work my head and shoulders in past the front of the door frame. Almost as soon as I was buckled in, it felt like we had been shot out of a cannon. "Don't tell me you were a race car driver in a previous life," I said, grinning.

"I take it that you haven't seen rush-hour traffic around here lately? Every second head start helps." Joan proceeded to take most turns on the side streets so fast I could have sworn only two wheels were in contact with the pavement. Upon arrival at the interstate highway ramp, she stomped on the accelerator to match the speed of the traffic flow.

6

A weather front moving through the Boston area created a heavy crosswind, which caused the plane to fishtail sideways while aiming for the short runway coming in for the over water approach to Logan Airport. With the wind shear factor, the pilot managed to do a three-point landing twice in an elapsed time of less than a minute.

I wasn't sure if Joan suffered any whiplash from being violently jerked in my direction, but it was awkward for me when my hands ended up on her chest to impede her lateral progress.

At least she appeared to be none the worse for wear after the second touchdown on the runway with full reverse thrusters and smoking brakes. The end of the runway was rushing at us at an alarming speed.

She looked up at me and calmly said, "Good catch, thank you," while ignoring exactly what part of her anatomy I caught to slow her down.

While the contact was not unpleasant, I must have blushed because my face felt warm when I said, "You're welcome." Perhaps I was embarrassed since we had just met or because she was so much younger. In any event, the brief encounter felt inappropriate. Maybe it was a combination of both, but I told myself I would make an extra effort to keep her at arms' length from now on.

There was no denying Joan was extremely well proportioned and physically fit, but the last thing I wanted was to initiate anything that could impede our progress on this case. I told myself, *Who knows? If we survive and this assignment works out well, there might be more government business for me down the road.*

After the plane taxied to the gate, the mechanical dong signaled we could stand at last and retrieve our carry-on luggage. I was surprised that Joan's bag weighed next to nothing as I handed it down to her. Most women I've had occasion to travel with always seemed reluctant to leave anything behind at home. If she could go on a trip without overpacking and still get the job done, then maybe we had more in common than I thought.

Gracefully weaving her way down the aisle on the plane, she looked like a filly exploding out of the starting gate at Belmont. We all but ran down the concourse to beat the crowd to the car rental booth in baggage claim. In full stride, she turned to tell me over her shoulder that she had made the reservation in her name since she was more familiar with the area. As I tried to keep up with her, I wondered why she wasn't out of breath since I was.

Hitting the lobby, she ignored the escalator, instead opting to run down the adjacent stairs. I wondered if she was just showing off because we'd already left our fellow passengers in the dust, but she only displayed a look of sheer determination. Another mental note to self, *Don't get in her way when she's concentrating.*

Unsurprisingly, we were the first to reach the rental counter with not another would-be customer in sight. In no time at all, we were across the street putting our luggage into the car. Getting into the passenger seat, I said, "Joan, I'm impressed with your efficiency, but there is no hurry. The rush-hour traffic has died down by now, so we've got plenty of time."

"I guess it's force of habit, Tom. The hotels in many of the countries I've traveled in tend to overbook. I just wanted to make sure they held our rooms for us," she said.

"Speaking of which, where are we staying tonight?" I asked.

"I made reservations at the Monticello Motor Inn on Route 9. It's located on what was once called the Golden Mile. Of course that was way back when they compared the entertainment available there to what Las Vegas had at the time. It's close to the Shoppers' World and a number of restaurants if you want to go out to eat after we check in," Joan said.

"I only had a sandwich for lunch today and a bag of peanuts on the plane, so I have worked up an appetite," I said, patting my tummy. There's a Hawaiian restaurant not too far down the street from there."

"I don't think I recall ever seeing a Hawaiian restaurant in the area, but that would be fine by me," she said, raising an eyebrow inquisitively.

"At least the traffic isn't backed up at the new Ted Williams Tunnel toll booths," I said as we approached the abbreviated queue. "I've always hated to try to catch a flight out of Logan Airport. One accident or a minor road repair can easily add an hour or two to the trip. It's hard to believe they can't arrange to have more flights out of a more central location like the Worcester or Westover airports. This place is only convenient to the ten percent of the passenger population who live in Boston."

"I know what you mean," Joan said. "When I lived in the area, I missed flights because I couldn't find a parking spot. There were also times when the Mass Port parking fees were more expensive than the cost of the round-trip airfare. Wow! I barely missed that huge pothole at the turnpike entrance ramp. A breakdown in the tunnel is all we'd need."

"Getting to and from the Hartford and Albany airports from the Berkshires is less of a hassle," I said. "The roads in western Massachusetts aren't in any better repair than the ones around Boston though."

"We don't have far to go. We get off at the Natick exit," Joan said. "These trips late in the day always seem to be more tiring."

I must have nodded off because Joan was giving my shoulder a nudge as she pulled into the motel driveway. "Are you in there, sleepyhead? Fine navigator you turned out to be," she said smiling.

"Sorry, it's been that kind of day. I didn't sleep yesterday and only caught a brief nap this morning. It's not the company. Shall we go sign in?" I asked, suppressing a yawn.

There was only one clerk on duty at the reservation desk. I let Joan check in first, but when she presented her identification, the clerk said, "That will be one room for two people for two nights."

Joan looked like she was trying to control her temper. Gritting her teeth together, she said, "The reservation says two rooms for two people for two nights. Please check again. Here is the confirmation."

"I'm sorry, there must be a glitch because our computer display doesn't agree with your confirmation. We only have one single room left," the clerk responded sheepishly.

Joan had calmed down, but one could tell she was not a happy camper the way she said, "I want to see your supervisor now!"

The clerk dialed a number and mumbled into the phone, explaining the situation. When the night manager showed up a few minutes later, he said, "I apologize for the confusion. The only other accommodation we have available is the honeymoon suite. We will make it available at the rate quoted for the single room."

"Wait a minute here. That is not acceptable either. Just because the reservations were made at the same time does not mean we are a couple. We reserved two separate rooms," Joan stated emphatically.

The manager looked surprised and said, "What you inferred is not what I meant. You are welcome to both the other room and the honeymoon suite at the rates originally quoted."

"That's more like it. Thank you for straightening this out. I hope you take a hard look at your reservation system so you don't give your other guests this much grief," Joan said. "May we have the room keys now, please?"

On the way back to the rental car, Joan said, "I hate when that happens. Would you like to go grab a bite to eat while I try to get my temper under control?"

"How could I resist such a sincere and heartwarming invitation?" I said with a grin.

"Do you want to flip to see who gets the suite?" Joan asked.

"I'm sure you would appreciate it much more than I would. Besides, you earned it back there," I said, glad she was on my side and not working against me.

"Now, where do we find this Hawaiian restaurant that you liked so much?" she asked.

"It's not far. Just take a left out of the driveway," I instructed with a straight face.

"There it is about a block further. Take your next left at the traffic light," I said.

"I don't see any Hawaiian restaurant," Joan said, frowning.

"It's right in front of you. See, the sign says 'Houlihan's.' They make a great burger," I said with a big grin.

"Very funny, I suppose they have green beer year around too," she remarked, breaking into a smile herself. At least she was a good sport about it.

Once our order was served and we were chowing down, I said to Joan, "So tell me how you got involved in this assignment."

Finishing off a French fry covered with ketchup, Joan replied, "It all started when we found an obsolete US short-range rocket in the DMZ in Korea. It obviously had been fired recently but didn't detonate. We had no record of any activity in the area. Upon dismantling, the bomb technicians were surprised to see computer parts from a late model Chevrolet modified to serve as a guidance system. I was part of a team called in because release of this type of technology to North Korea was verboten."

"Was this kind of finding an isolated case?" I asked.

"No, in bits and pieces, we discovered the North Koreans were using components of US developed designs in weapons taken from microwave oven switches, sensors from clothes driers, TV tuners, et cetera, et cetera," Joan said, tentatively eyeing the dessert menu before putting it down. "In turn, they were selling this modified weapons technology to countries like Iran and Pakistan."

"What did they do with all the appliances and equipment with the missing parts?"

"They replaced the high-tech switches and controls with old-fashioned, conventional units to resell the donor parent appliance, tool, or whatever. Complete assembly lines were set up to rebuild the finished products, so nothing would go to waste and the evidence disappeared," Joan said.

"Obviously, they felt Peter Pickering was getting too close to discovering the details of what they were up to," I said, trying not to talk with my mouth full.

"He was in a perfect position to keep track of who was doing what and how many units were involved since he was supplying the distributors and the Asian trading companies. They in turn were reselling the old style replacement sub-assemblies," she said as she sipped her coffee.

Joan held up her credit card as the waitress walked by and asked, "Could you put half of our charges on my card, please?"

I fumbled to get out my wallet and said, "Please put the other half of the bill on this card. Thank you."

The waitress raised an eyebrow and looked us over. Apparently she was trying to figure out exactly who this odd couple was and why they were doing the Dutch treat routine.

It was Saturday night, but it didn't appear to be a date. She was obviously younger, but it couldn't have looked like I could be her dad unless she was adopted. Accepting both cards, she smiled, shrugged, and headed toward the kitchen to do her thing since we didn't ask for dessert or more coffee.

"Didn't Alex explain all of this before you accepted the assignment?" Joan asked.

"He did. I just wanted to hear it from your perspective and how you became involved. I did manage to glean a number or pieces of new information from you that Alex didn't cover, so it was a very worthwhile exercise as far as I'm concerned. Thank you for indulging me," I said.

We signed our credit card slips for the meal, and Joan drove back to the motel. We retrieved our bags from the trunk and headed for the side door of the motel. The directions for using the key card had been painted over so it took a couple of trial swipes to open the outside door. As we parted company at the elevator, I said, "My room is just down that corridor. Sleep well. By the way, what time do you want to meet for breakfast?"

Pushing the up button, Joan said, "I would think 9:00 AM would be early enough to get everything done if we can get a hold of Lucille. Good night, Tom."

7

After I knocked on the door of the honeymoon suite, I greeted Joan with "Good morning, sunshine."

"Bah, humbug," Joan responded, barely breaking into a smile.

"I assume that means you didn't rest well last night?" I inquired.

"No, the message light was flashing on my phone when I got to the suite. My dad said he called my office when he couldn't reach me on my cell phone. I must not have turned it back on when we arrived at the airport yesterday. The office wasn't supposed to tell anyone where I was, but they gave him the phone number of the motel because he said it was a family emergency," she said.

"I'm sorry to hear that. Is everyone all right?" I inquired, concerned.

"Everything is fine except for my father. He claimed he was worried because I cut him off when we talked yesterday. When he called the motel, they told him I was staying in the bridal suite, but I was out at the moment. That caused him to go through the roof," Joan said. "I honestly don't know what I'm going to do with him. I'm thirty years old, and he tries to treat me like I'm still a teenager. I told him I can take care of myself, and he should get a hobby that doesn't involve me. Then I hung up on him."

"Other than that, how is your morning going so far?" I asked, chuckling to myself.

"I'm tempted to knock your block off for that remark. You are not helping my mood one bit," she said as she stepped back with her arms folded, glaring at me.

"On the more positive side, I did manage to contact Lucille this morning. We're going to meet her at Peter's office on Union Street in Framingham at 11:00 AM. That gives us plenty of time to grab breakfast at IHOP and a Sunday paper," I said, trying to suppress a smile. "By the way, I like your accommodations."

"Oh, shut up," Joan said as she pushed me out into the corridor and slammed the door shut behind us.

Once we were in the elevator, I said, "If it's any consolation, I know exactly how your dad feels. I try not to be overprotective of my daughter, but it isn't easy. She knows I love her and can rely on her judgment. It's just the guys she encounters that I don't trust, but I can't keep her wrapped up in a bubble."

"Yeah, I know, but we've been through this over and over again. He just doesn't get it. I don't know what the solution is," Joan said.

"Do you think he would relax a little if I were to talk to him? I could assure him I don't have any designs on his little girl," I suggested hesitantly.

"Heck no, that wouldn't make him feel any better. It would probably only make things worse. Let's leave well enough alone," she said, unlocking the car.

Pulling into the IHOP parking lot, I said, "At least there doesn't appear to be much of a line waiting for tables."

It wasn't long before we were seated with cups of steaming hot coffee. I asked for the Lumberjack Special while Joan was more conservative with her order of the Split Decision Combo.

Few words were exchanged as we enjoyed our breakfast. The crowd started to thin out, so we didn't feel bad about nursing more coffee while we browsed through the *Metro West* newspaper I had picked up from the dispenser outside. I wondered why anyone would want the name of a newspaper associated with crime, corruption, and congestion of a city instead of calling it Country East. After all, the country is where all the city folk go to unwind from all the stress of city life. Most employees live in the suburbs and put up with the hassle of commuting in and out of the city every day.

"I guess we should pay the bill and head out to meet Lucille," I said, not wanting to get up out of the seat.

"You go ahead and start without me, Tom, I'm too full to move," Joan said with a half smile, slowly pushing her chair back.

Turning into the Three P Company parking lot, a car coming from the opposite direction pulled up from behind us. A tall, thin woman in a business suit with graying hair pulled severely back into a bun got out of her car and approached us. I walked over to meet her and said, "Hi, I'm Tom Powers, you must be Lucille. This is my associate Joan Walters. Thank you for coming out on a Sunday."

Shaking hands, Lucille said, "How do you do? I'll do anything I can to help Mr. Pickering. He is a wonderful man and a very dear friend."

We followed Lucille in after she unlocked the door and hurried to turn off the alarm. Facing us, she asked, "How can I help?"

"We can start by looking for Peter Pickering's journal in his office. Do you have any idea what it looks like?" I asked.

"Certainly, it's a light blue, hardcover, lined, blank book. The dimensions are about nine by twelve inches, but I haven't seen it in a while," Lucille said as she unlocked the inner door and led us into his office. "I suspect he took it with him or brought it home."

"I assume Monique explained we are trying to retrace his steps to find out where he'd been and who he had contacted recently," I said. "Do you have a copy of his latest itinerary, Lucille?"

"No, he usually takes care of making all his reservations for himself. He frequently would leave an area or country as soon as he completed his business there. Then he'd contact the next company he planned to see on that particular trip," Lucille said. "He felt he could be more efficient that way."

Looking through his desk for clues, Joan held up an odd-shaped gold key and asked, "Do you happen to know what this key fits?"

"I have never seen that key before, so I have no idea," Lucille responded. "It certainly doesn't go to anything in the office."

"In that case, I'll bring it with us to the Pickering home to see if it belongs there," Joan said as she put it in her pocket.

"Forgive me. I don't know where my manners are. Would you care for a cup of coffee if I were to brew a pot?" Lucille said.

"Thanks for the kind offer, but if I have one more cup of coffee this morning, I'll float out of here. We just came from having breakfast at the International House of Pancakes," I said. "When we finish an examination of what's in Peter's office, I'm sure we will have more questions about the business to ask you later, however."

"Of course, I will catch up on some paperwork in the meantime," Lucille said as she walked out to her desk.

"I've completed a review of all the desk contents. I'll start on the file cabinet while you go through the bookcase,"

Joan said. "Peter is very neat and well organized. There really doesn't appear to be much that will give us the kind of clues we need."

"The only thing I've found so far that looks unusual is a piece of paper that could be just used as a bookmark, but it has a series of numbers on it. They might be safe combinations, phone numbers, account numbers, or longitude and latitudes," I said to Joan, walking out to Lucille's desk. "Lucille, could you please make a copy of this? I'll put the original back where I found it."

Lucille handed me the original and copy of the note. Inserting it back into the book on *Value Added Tax, International Practice and Problems* by Alan A. Tait, I couldn't see anything germane the scrap of paper was marking in a section that said the VAT in Switzerland is 8 percent.

I understood that Peter spoke seven languages fluently, so all the translation dictionaries in multiple languages didn't surprise me. Apparently he dealt with exporting to many different countries around the globe. Likewise, it would explain all the novels in different languages with well wishes penned and autographed in the flyleaves.

Not finding anything in the bookcase pertinent to the purpose of our visit, I turned to Joan and said, "Other than the note, there was nothing out of the ordinary over here. How are you doing in the file cabinet?"

Joan turned but kept her hand on the folder she was examining to keep her place. She responded, "All the invoices and correspondence only mention the distributor or trading company. I haven't found any reference to a customer, end user, destination or application. That seems extremely odd. Peter's journal could shed some light on that if we can ever locate it. I'm almost done here."

"In that case, I'll ask Lucille about that and to supply us with a complete list of their customers and contacts," I said.

Returning to find Lucille busy at her desk, I inquired if she knew of any of the end uses that the Three P Company products went into or who the ultimate purchasers were.

"Almost all the requests for quotes that come in are for specific part numbers. Many are for obsolete components. The quantities are appreciable enough for our suppliers to make dedicated, full-scale production runs efficiently though," Lucille said. "I don't think that we ever knew what the applications were or who the components were shipped to after leaving the distributors' loading docks. Since our terms were either cash in advance or upon delivery, it didn't matter to us."

"Do you know of any supplier or Three P customer who might have been upset with Peter?" I asked.

"Absolutely not, Peter was well liked by everyone we did business with. Any time there was a delay or a product damaged in shipment, Peter would see to it personally to make sure the problem was resolved so it wouldn't happen again," Lucille said.

At that moment, Joan joined us in the open office area. She said, "I'm finished in there."

"Lucille, could you please make a copy of the Three P customer list for us by tomorrow?" I asked. "By the way, what does the Three P Company name stand for?"

Lucille responded, "When Mr. Pickering was trying to decide what to name the company, he didn't want to leave anything out. Because he represented so many diversified commodities, he finally settled on Peter Pickering's Parts or the Three P Company.

"Lucille, thank you very much for everything. You have been extremely helpful. We will return early tomorrow morning to talk to the other employees as a group," I said as we picked up our notes to leave. "What would be a good time to do that?"

"Anytime after we open at 8:00 AM would be fine," she replied.

The next day, we met at length with the rest of the Three P workers. Without exception, no one had any idea who the end users were, the final destinations of the products or the end use applications. It was assumed by everyone that discretion regarding the details of their customers' businesses was an unwritten Three P policy, so no questions were ever asked.

After thanking the employees for their time while avoiding discussions of where Peter Pickering might be, we obtained the Three P customer list from Lucille and thanked her for all the help. Perhaps I was surprised Lucille didn't ask about Peter, but maybe she felt it wasn't her place if the information wasn't offered freely.

The weather report for the Berkshires said the snow storm had passed and it was cold but sunny as we set out headed west on the Massachusetts Turnpike.

8

The opaque white ice cascading out of the dark rock ledges at the highest point on the Massachusetts pike at 1725 feet above sea level in the town of Becket made us glad to be enveloped in the warmth emanating from the rental car heater.

The music of the intermittent signal sneaking between the mountain peaks from the FM radio stations helped to drown out the howling of the wind that threatened to snap the swaying trees as we approached the top of the mountain.

With two of us exhaling, the defroster needed to be turned on occasionally. The warm air blowing in my face tended to lull me to sleep. Fortunately, I wasn't driving.

"Have you ever shopped at the Lee Premium Outlets?" I asked Joan as we crested the peak and descended toward exit 2 on US Route 20.

"No, we had too many shopping malls in eastern Massachusetts when I lived in that area," Joan replied. "It's a wonder there are enough shopaholics to keep them all in business. Since I resigned my army commission, I haven't had time to round out my wardrobe. As a former tomboy, I was never a clothes-horse kind of gal, though."

"From what I've seen so far, your tastes are impeccable," I said, wondering if I should have kept that observation to myself.

"Why, thank you, Tom. You look kinda cute yourself for an old guy. At least your mother doesn't dress you funny when you leave the house," she said with a chuckle. "I'm just glad my dad isn't listening in on this conversation. He'd be having another conniption."

We headed west at the exit on US Route 20 and then turned north after a few miles towards the town of Westmoreland off Route 7. The plows had cleared the highways well. Between the combined effects of the salt, sand, and the sun, the roads weren't the least bit slippery. Driving up the unplowed entrance to the Pickering estate, we noticed tire marks in the snow and footprints leading to the front of the house.

I always feel naked without my gun when I take trips on a plane. This was one of those times I wished I had one with me. We approached the front cautiously, to find the door ajar with the frame shattered because someone had pried the deadbolt open.

I started to go in first, but Joan slipped past me. I was just going to say something when I notice a red laser dot on her chest. Pushing her out of the way on reflex, I felt a sharp pain pierce my shoulder on my way down.

Joan immediately dropped to my side. Then we heard a door slam and an engine start up followed by a loud crash. By the time Joan helped me up, we could only see a dark sedan swerving out of the end of the drive. Pieces of the splintered garage door were strewn about near the house. The license plate was too far away to read.

I was feeling a little woozy when Joan asked if I could stand okay for a minute. Not sure, I said, "I'm all right," anyway. It was then I realized I didn't hear the report of the gun. The shooter must have been using a silencer.

I turned to see Joan dash into the powder room down the hall and emerge with a couple of towels. She carefully removed my coat and shirt while I dripped blood on the light beige living room rug.

"At least the bullet didn't hit a major artery and went all the way through your shoulder," she said as she applied towels to the entrance and exit wounds. "Let's get you lying down again so I can call for help and find something to wrap your shoulder with."

Joan carefully lowered me back to the floor while holding a towel in the front and one in back of my shoulder. Grabbing my right hand and placing it over the towel on top, she said, "There, keep pressure on that."

I shivered with the wind blowing in the front doorway, so Joan covered me with my coat and walked over to close the door. It immediately blew open again, so she propped the cast iron umbrella rack against it as she reached to find her cell phone. "Nine-one-one, what is the nature of your emergency?" the voice on the other end said, loud enough for me to hear.

"This is Joan Walters. We have a man with a gunshot wound to the shoulder at the home of Peter Pickering at 257 Mountain Road in Westmoreland. Please send an ambulance immediately." Joan nodded her head and said, "Okay," and terminated the call.

"They'll be here in about fifteen minutes. Don't move, I'll be right back," she said over her shoulder as she ran down the hall again.

Upon returning, Joan said, "These silk sheets are the best thing I could find in the linen closet."

Joan acted like it was painful to rip the fine silk into long strips to snuggly hold the towels wrapped around me enough to slow the bleeding. "It seems a shame to tear expensive sheets up like this, so I hope you're worth it," she said, grinning.

"Since I didn't mention it yet, thank you for saving my life. By the way, I heard an ancient Chinese proverb says, 'If you save a person's life, they are your responsibility forever,'" Joan said, still smiling.

I winced when she tightened up the ends to tie them off. "In that case, I won't repeat that last bit of information to your father, should I ever meet him," I said, groaning.

"Good plan. We'll leave the 'I've got you, babe' routine to Sonny and Cher as well," she said.

"Before I forget, could you please take the cell phone out of my jacket and call my cousin Janyce? She's on the Westmoreland Police Force. Explain what happened, ask her to come over to dust for prints, and have her call Jerry at the Quaboag Police Department to give her a hand," I said. "I suspect the security systems and cameras were disabled, but maybe they can find something useful anyway."

Completing the phone call, Joan was kneeling by my side when we heard the ambulance pull up with the siren wailing. She stretched enough to see over the sill of the bay window. "The EMTs are here, wheeling in a gurney," Joan said. "I'll move the umbrella stand out of the way for them."

As they took off my coat and started to unwrap the temporary dressing Joan had applied, I winced from the pain. Maybe I was getting used to it the way it was. The EMT pulled out a hypodermic syringe. I asked, "What is that for?"

He said, "To control the pain."

In my best impression of a Bronx accent, I said, "Forget about it."

Joan said, "Don't be a baby, it's only a quick injection."

"I'd rather be fully conscious and alert when Janyce and Jerry show up so I can talk to them," I said.

As if on cue, they appeared at the door almost simultaneously. Janyce said, "Tom, are you okay?"

"I will be with a little rest and recuperation after I get patched up," I said. "Why don't you and Jerry go into the dining room so Joan can explain to you what this is all about while I get my shoulder properly wrapped?"

The EMTs were finishing up when Joan reappeared from the dining room. "Jerry and Janyce are all set to dust for prints, check the security systems, look for the journal, and have the doors repaired. Janyce will ask the Westmoreland Police to do extra patrols in this area to watch the house in case the home invaders try to come back," she said. "I'll follow the ambulance to the hospital."

"Don't you have this 'Confucius says' thing backward?" I said. "I thought I was supposed to be responsible for you from now on, not the other way around."

"You've already demonstrated a propensity for jumping in front of tiny objects moving at much higher rates of speed than you are capable of attaining. If it happens again on my watch, how would I explain it to Alex? He might believe the first time you got shot was not my fault, but if it happened twice? Not so much. Don't forget, as a hired gun, you're not on the company payroll so we can't cover the medical costs," Joan said.

"There's nothing you can do at the hospital. Why don't you stay here to help Janyce and Jerry?" I said.

"There's no way that's going to happen, compadre. You took a bullet that was meant for me. The least I can do is make sure you are properly repaired. Jerry and Janyce have everything under control. I'd just be in the way here. Let's go get you taken care of first, then we'll figure out what our next step will be," Joan said as she followed the gurney out through the broken door frame.

Joan managed to keep up with the ambulance all the way through every red light in the city of Quaboag to get to the Berkshire Medical Center Hospital. By the time I had a clerk filling out the medical insurance forms, she burst through the ER doors out of breath. Looking around, she spotted me in the corner and came over to sit quietly until the paperwork was completed.

"Everyone in this town must get sick at the same time. I had to troll all the way to the other end of the parking lot to find an empty space," Joan said as a man in a business suit with a badge on his belt came over to the gurney.

"They said at the desk you are Tom Powers. I'm Captain Bill Potter of the Massachusetts State Police. Your old partner Jerry called about a shooting you were involved in," he said.

"I'll take care of the report," Joan said to the officer. "I was there too. Besides, that doctor looks like he's headed this way to take care of Tom. Please make certain that our names don't get published because the shooter is still out there, and he or she doesn't need to know who we are."

The guy in the white coat introduced himself as Dr. Gosh. He reviewed the chart and had the attendant wheel me into an ER station before closing the curtain.

9

They must have put me totally under with a general anesthetic because I felt extremely groggy. When I awoke, there was a beautiful dark angel sitting by the bed with the most gorgeous smile I'd ever seen, radiating a warm glow.

"It's about time you woke up. Fine partner you turned out to be. All you do is sleep on the job," she said.

"Oh…hi, it's you, Joan. I'm just trying to get my bearings. What's going on?" I asked, wondering why I felt drawn to her all of a sudden.

Outside, the sky was mostly overcast with a few stars twinkling between the opaque clouds. My shoulder felt very stiff and sore, like they drove a Mac truck over it.

"The doctor said you were extremely lucky. If the bullet had hit just a few millimeters in any direction, you could have had serious complications. It turns out your recuperation time won't be that bad either, but you will need extensive physical therapy on your shoulder muscles," Joan said, probably wondering why I was staring at her.

"Did they say how long I will have to stay in the hospital?"

"About a week to keep it immobilized and make certain there's no chance of infection," she said.

"How come they told you all of this?"

"When I explained to them I was your daughter, they looked at me funny, so I said you had adopted me when I was young," Joan said. "While you were in surgery, I returned the car to the rental agency. Janyce came over to bring me back to the hospital. Then she went with Jerry to your apartment to bring your car here."

"You sure have been one busy little beaver. Did they say what they found at the Pickering estate?" I asked.

"Janyce pulled a number of fingerprints, but it will take a while to find out who they belong to. We'll need prints from Monique, Peter, and the cleaning service people for reference," she said. "The mess from the break-in was concentrated in the study and in front of the bookcase in the living room, but they probably were wearing gloves. There's no way of knowing what the intruder was looking for or what was taken. Maybe we interrupted him, her, or them before they found what they were after."

"Was there any clue from the security tapes on who they were or which area they were focusing on first?" I asked.

"A lone figure in a hooded parka could be seen walking up the drive before the wires were cut and the systems shut down. The footprints in the snow out front were on the small side, so they could have been made by a woman or a small man. They were too drifted in with snow to be able to tell," Joan explained. "There was no sign of the journal, but with the attention paid to the bookcase and small spaces, they could have been searching for Peter's book."

"What about the clues from the Three P Company office in Framingham?" I asked.

"The key from Peter's desk in Framingham didn't appear to fit anything there. We can check with Monique and the cleaning service to see if they recognize the key. Jerry and Janyce didn't see anything that would explain what all the numbers on the bookmark note meant. We can ask Monique if she knows anything about that as well," Joan said.

I must have held my stare at Joan too long because she asked, "Were you about to say or ask about something else?"

Forcing myself to avoid eye contact, I said, "I was thinking of something I wanted to ask you, but it slipped my mind. It seemed important at the time, but maybe it's a residual effect from the anesthesia."

"Unless I can get you a cup of coffee or something to eat, I'm going to go have dinner myself, since I missed lunch today. I only wanted to wait to see if you needed anything and to make sure you were okay after surgery," Joan said.

"No, there's nothing I can think of at the moment. I just feel very sleepy. Thank you for staying to let me know all the particulars," I said. "I'm certain I'll feel better in the morning, so I'd appreciate it if you could bring me a change of clothes and a gun for each of us tomorrow from my place. I'd like to leave here right after I have a chance to talk to the doctor. I want us to be prepared the next time we run into trouble. Janyce has a key to my apartment."

"Tom, you won't be any help to me if you leave before you're ready and have a relapse. We'll see if the doctor thinks you're fit to be discharged when I come back here tomorrow," she said.

"Thank you for your concern, but it's not like I haven't been shot before. If it feels better I can have them put my wing in a sling and be on my way," I said. "I'll bet you just want to make sure I could hold up my end of the bargain to be responsible for you."

"I can see I'm going to have a long talk with your cousin Janyce to find out if you've always been this pig headed and stubborn. Good night," Joan said with a big smile as she turned to go.

"Good night, Joan," I said, wondering exactly why she looked so much more appealing tonight. Maybe I was just beginning to notice.

This is crazy, I told myself again. *She is much too young for me (or is it that I'm entirely too old for her?). I don't want to get involved with anyone. She's working with me on this one case, and I may never see her again after that. I need to keep my head clear, and I can't get involved with anyone. Still, she is adorable.*

10

The clock on the wall said 6:00 AM as the nurse dropped off a breakfast tray. I don't think she was the same one that woke me from a sound sleep at 3:00 AM to ask if I needed another pain pill so I could sleep better.

It was hard enough to find a position that was even remotely comfortable so I could relax the first time. I kept tossing and turning for what seemed like forever before I finally succumbed to sleep. "You are what you eat," I told the earlier nurse on the graveyard shift after refusing the pill. That caused her to go off in a huff. Then I desperately tried to get back to my place in dreamland where I left off prior to the rude interruption.

It's funny that you take the concept of having two arms for granted until you lose the use of one of them. The breakfast sausage served with the scrambled eggs must have been made with natural casing, because it was too tough to cut with just a fork without it sliding off the plate.

With my right arm, I would be able spear a link with my fork and bite it off, but then I'd have an impaled sausage that I couldn't easily get off the fork. The obvious choice was to keep chewing on it until I finished a link.

It was either that or I would have had to convince one of the nurses to cut my food for me, and I'm too macho a guy to ask anyone to do that. Besides, they all look so darn young. Does that mean I'm officially at middle age or worse yet, over the hill? Perhaps the younger ones with low seniority get stuck on the night shift.

Since I'm right handed, if I had to get shot, I should be glad that it was in the left shoulder. I could eat left-handed, but I definitely shoot and write better with my right hand.

Another problem was that I found it difficult to get the runny eggs all the way up to my mouth while sitting in a half-reclining position. Strategic placement of the burnt toast on the plate backed up by the water glass on the tray allowed me to transfer the eggs to the fork. I just had to sneak up on them carefully by leaning forward just enough to avoid pulling on the stitches. The rest was just careful balance.

It's a good thing that they supplied napkins with me being this messy. Who knew that breakfast could be so difficult? If I were staying here, I could order cereal tomorrow. Hopefully I wouldn't have to cut that, but with hospital and army food, one never knows.

No sooner than I had finished eating, when Joan's bodacious smiling face appeared in the doorway.

"Good morning, bright eyes. You look lovely this morning," I said.

"If you'll pardon me for saying so, you still look terrible, partner," Joan said cheerfully. "It looks like I'm too late for you to have your Dunkin' Donuts coffee with your breakfast. Because you were a cop at one time, I figured you'd also need doughnuts with that. I brought you a decaf since you still need your rest to recuperate. I decided that you couldn't handle a powdered jelly donut with one hand, but you might want to try to dunk these two old-fashioned, plain doughnuts. If you have trouble with that, I can always cut them up so you can eat them with a fork."

"You're timing couldn't be better," I said. "Thank you very much. I think what they call coffee here is a mixture of vinegar, crank case oil, and a little shoe polish. It tastes horrible. They still haven't got the Starbucks' burnt essence flavor right though. I'm sure I can manage the donuts just fine by myself."

"Your two hand guns are out in the trunk of your car. I have the change of clothes you asked for here," she said with a disapproving frown as she tossed the red gym bag on the visitor's chair in the corner. "First, we'll see what the doctor has to say about the possibility of you leaving," Joan said with her voice lowered and more than a hint of exasperation in it.

"Now you sound like my mother. I feel a little better today. Or at least I did until I tried a cup of that hospital coffee."

The nurse returned to collect my tray; eyeing the remains of the doughnut in my hand and the crumbs I had managed to scatter everywhere. "Excuse me, what time does the doctor make his rounds?" I asked anxiously, half to distract her from the mess I made with the doughnut.

"Dr. Gosh had emergency surgery to perform so he won't be by this morning. A Dr. Broz will be filling in for him. I believe she should be here within the hour," the nurse responded with a cluck and a wrinkled brow.

"Thank you. Would you please round up the appropriate paperwork so I can sign out of here when the doctor shows up?" I asked.

"I'm afraid it will be up to the doctor to decide when you are ready to leave," she informed me in what I think was supposed to sound like an authoritative tone.

"No, it's my decision. I can sign out even if it's against the doctor's advice. Please have the paperwork ready along with an extra left-handed sling. Thank you," I said as pleasantly as I could muster while flashing my boyish smile before the nurse did an abrupt about face and all but ran out the door shaking her head.

"You sure have a way with women. I take it you've never read the book *How to Win Friends and Influence People*," Joan said with a big grin, showing off her pearly whites.

"First things first," I said as I cautiously slid off the bed to the floor while being careful not to move my shoulder any more than absolutely necessary. "Please, hand me my pants so I can get out of this Johnny."

I went into the bathroom, determined to do dress myself without help. I was able to step into my pants with both feet. Bracing myself for what was to come next; I held my left arm gingerly against my chest and gritted my teeth. I managed to do a deep knee bend while steadily pulling on the waist band to snake my pants past my knees by shifting my weight back and forth from one foot to the other.

Standing up ever so slowly, I buttoned the waist with my right hand. With that accomplished, I somehow pulled up the zipper. I waited for the throbbing pain and lightheadedness to subside a bit before returning to the room to face Joan.

Backing up to the bed, I stood on my tiptoes to raise my rear end enough to sit down on the mattress. Reaching for the metal frame at the head of the bed with my good arm, I swung my feet up on the mattress while keeping my torso as rigid as possible to drag my butt up the rest of the way.

"You sure are fun to watch. That was very graceful for a dude," Joan said sarcastically. "It doesn't look to me like you'll be ready to leave anytime soon, but then again, what do I know?"

"At least I don't feel a draft from the slit in the Johnny," I retorted, knowing she was probably right. Then I added, "I'm sorry. I appreciate all your help. I'm just frustrated."

"Hey, it's okay. If it hadn't been for you, it could be me in the hospital bed instead of you, or I might be dead," she said, looking genuinely grateful as she gently reached over to touch my good arm.

It only took one look back into those beautiful brown eyes to make me realize I was going to have to be more discrete in veiling any feelings I might have for this talented and capable young woman. I would be seriously tempted by her if I were ten or fifteen years younger.

Just then, a doctor entered the room to save me from the possibility of making a fool of myself any further than I already have.

"Good morning, I'm Dr. Broz, filling in for Dr. Gosh," she said with a friendly smile. "Let me take a minute to see what your chart looks like."

"Hi, I'm Tom Powers and this is my daughter Joan. It's a pleasure to meet you. I'd like to arrange to check out as soon as possible today," I said.

"From what I can determine, your vital statistics are all in the range we'd like to see, but we don't recommend leaving this soon after you've had such a traumatic incident," the doctor said. "You could develop an infection or put stress on your stitches before the incisions have had a chance to begin to heal."

"Dr. Broz, I appreciate your concern, but I've had bullet wounds much worse than this before. I've always been quick to mend, but I will exercise extreme caution and follow all your instructions to the letter," I said. "I feel I can recuperate much faster in my own bed while eating my own food. Besides, my daughter here is a stern taskmaster and will make certain that I will receive appropriate care."

After she removed the sling and hospital Johnny, she started to gently pull off the tapes. Dr. Broz said, "I can't say that would be the best way to get you back on your feet without a relapse, but let me finish removing the bandages and see what it looks like."

"There's no sign of infection or external bleeding. Can you lift your arm at all?" she asked.

I tried to oblige, surprised that I was so stiff that I couldn't lift my left arm above my shoulder.

"That's good. How about forward and backward range of motion, ever so slowly? Stop if you feel pulling on your stitches."

I was surprised that I could move my elbow forward about six inches, but only back a couple without flinching accompanied by intense pain.

"It looks good to me so far. You can rest your arm on your lap while I replace the bandages. It would look much better after a week in a controlled hospital environment with a gradual scale up of activity along with physical therapy. Are you absolutely certain I can't convince you to stay here for at least a few more days?" the doctor asked.

As she applied fresh dressings to the wounds, I said, "No, Dr. Broz. Just between us girls, we may be in danger if the home invaders that shot me found out who and where we are. It would also be safer for everyone at the hospital if we get out of here right away. I would appreciate it if my name were to disappear from the hospital records for this incident. If there are any questions, contact Captain Bill Potter of the Massachusetts State Police or Detective Jerry Ford at the Quaboag Municipal Police Department. I will return in ten days to have the stitches removed. Thank you again."

The doctor did not look very pleased, but she reluctantly signed the release forms duly noting it was against doctor's advice. "You know I could get in trouble bending the hospital rules like this, so you better make sure I'm not sorry." Then she called to have an orderly take me down the elevator in a wheelchair to the main entrance.

Joan had already gone to get my car and pulled in front to pick me up at the door. She ran around the car to help me into the passenger's side with a concerned look on her face. Getting back behind the wheel, she said, "I didn't think that we could still be a target for the shooter."

"The intruder took off in a hurry and probably doesn't know that one of us was shot. He or she also can't be certain if we can identify them. We don't need an article in the newspaper or a police report with our names on it to make it easier for them find us either," I said.

"How are you doing?" Joan asked.

"Maybe I'm getting too old for this, because it hurts like crazy this time," I said. "Please try to go around the bigger pot holes and frost heaves."

Approaching the exit to the parking lot, Joan asked, "Where are we going now?"

"Head north on Route 7 and stop at the first motel vacancy sign you see. They may not know who or where we are, but we'll stay away from my place for the time being just in case. We know what they did to Peter. There's no point in taking any chances."

"Please slow down a little more. That bullet must have torn up more tissue in my shoulder than I thought it did."

"There's a vacancy sign at the Pontoosic Motel on the right. Park in the back with the car out of sight and see if they have two adjoining rooms or at least two that are adjacent. If there is a choice, the preference would be in the back, away from the highway. Tell them I'm a light sleeper and don't like traffic noise if they should ask."

Joan returned to the car and said, "They've got two rooms in back on the first floor with a common doorway between them. One room has a kitchenette. Both have Internet access so we can use the Virtual Private Network for our communications."

"That's great. We'll get set up and contact Alex as soon as we can find out how far Jerry and Janyce have progressed with the investigation. We just crossed the Lanesboro town line. Give them a call and have them meet us for lunch at Friendly's Restaurant across the street at noon. Since the bad guys may have written down the rental car license plate number, we'd better not use your last name from now on, just in case. I'll sign in at the office with my credit card and you'll be my adopted daughter, Joan Powers," I said.

"You really are taking this Chinese thing seriously about being responsible for me now, aren't you?" Joan asked, breaking into one of her trademark big grins.

"Stop being a wise cracker. I want to figure out how to keep them from finding out who we are before we can determine their identities and who is behind all this," I said, trying to look less concerned than I really was. Now come around to my side and help me ease out of the car very slowly," I said. "All those bumps and potholes you hit on the way here were extremely painful. Next time, you can at least try to go around a few of them. I need to lie down to rest for a little while before we meet Janyce and Jerry."

"I'm sorry, Tom. I didn't know you were that bad off. I'll try to be more careful when I drive from now on."

Joan helped me to lie down slowly on the bed and prop my shoulder up with an extra pillow before returning to her room and quietly closing the door.

11

After I had a little nap, I felt slightly better. Joan wanted me to take a pain pill, but I didn't want to be sleepy while we decided on a course of action. We walked across the street to meet Janyce and Jerry for lunch at the Friendly's Restaurant.

We knew they had arrived before we did since Janyce's Jeep and Jerry's unmarked police car were already parked out in front. Joan raced a couple of steps ahead to open the door for me, grinning.

"What did I say before about not being a wise guy? I'm sore, not a total invalid," I said as we entered and saw them both seated in a large booth in the back with Captain Bill Potter of the Massachusetts State Police.

I leaned toward Joan and quietly said, "Would you please pull up a chair to the table? Sliding into the booth may not be a good thing for me. I also don't want to take a chance of anyone bumping into my shoulder."

I was surprised to see Bill but realized he must be helping out Jerry by getting some of the tests run at the state laboratory facilities. "Don't get up," I said. "I probably shouldn't lean across the table to shake hands. Thank you for coming. Why don't we place our orders for lunch and then we can talk."

"At the speed you're moving today, you might be able to order off the Senior Menu and get away with it," Jerry cracked. "How do you feel?"

"Like I've been violated. How do you think I feel? The last time I was shot was when I was younger and more resilient back in my army days. Otherwise the shoulder is still very sore. Are you ganging up on me with Joan by picking on the guy that's broken?" I asked. "By the way, the rental car we used was in Joan's name, so for the time being, she's my adopted daughter Joan Powers. That might slow down anyone trying to find out who we are."

Looking over the menu, I was surprised to see there were in fact special offerings for seniors on the back page. I'd probably never noticed it before since I usually ordered a full meal from the middle of the menu unless I was in a hurry and settled for a sandwich. Until my shoulder heals enough to exercise again, I'll have to cut down on my caloric intake.

Once we'd ordered and had our coffees poured, I said, "What did we learn from the Pickering estate crime scene so far?"

As he sipped his coffee, Jerry said, "I studied the short bit of recording from the security cameras before the power was cut. From the footprint in the snow, gait, and size of the hooded figure, I'm convinced it had to be a small woman. I couldn't find any recent record of a female shooter in western Massachusetts, so she might have been from outside of the area. Since we could not find any fingerprints that didn't belong to the Pickerings or their cleaning staff, we don't know how many people were involved in the break in. They must have been wearing gloves."

"Did you get any leads from the bullet?" I asked.

"We couldn't find any record of nine-millimeter bullets with the same striations. With the laser sight and silencer, we suspect that particular alloy was probably fired by a Beretta model 92FS. It's a fairly common weapon. Many police departments use it instead of buying from domestic manufacturers like Colt or Smith & Wesson," Bill said.

"Can we tell if anything was taken?" I asked.

"Everything was in such disarray that we assumed they were frustrated because they couldn't find whatever they were looking for before being interrupted by you and Joan," Janyce said.

"Did you verify that our names are not on any of the police reports and hospital lists?" I asked.

"Taken care of. I also made arrangements for repairs to the house and garage. The company that supplied the security system installed several upgrades to make the alarms and sensors much more difficult for them to be incapacitated. I asked the Westmoreland chief of police to increase the frequency of patrols in the area too," Janyce replied with her usual efficiency.

"How about the threatening note Monique received in the mail?" I asked.

Bill said, "The crime lab exposed the letter and envelope in a cyanoacrylate cloud chamber but couldn't raise any latent fingerprints. Minute traces of acryonitrile on the envelope suggested talc-free gloves were used that are common to hospitals and clean rooms for electronics manufacturing. The dimensions of the paper were a metric size normally used in Europe, but the note was mailed locally.

"Some of the colors in the glued on printed letters that formed the message were obsolete at Sandoz before they merged to become Clariant in Muttenz, Switzerland. The adhesive used to stick the letters on the note employed a base polymer from Henkel in Dusseldorf, Germany.

"The high-gloss paper underneath the printing had a burnished clay barrier coating for ink hold out, so we think they were from upscale European magazines printed in the last few years. That says the threat to Monique was mailed locally by someone with access to European paper stock, magazines, and adhesives."

"It seems they might have sent a professional from Europe to threaten Monique and keep an eye on her. I'll have to ask Alex to keep her in protective custody and restrict her contacts with outside people," I said.

"Did you and Joan make any progress on the case at the Three P Company office in Framingham?" Jerry asked.

"We came up with an odd-shaped key from Peter Pickering's office desk that didn't belong to anything there. On a hunch, I borrowed a phone directory at the hospital. The only area bank that advertises safe deposit boxes was Berkshire Savings and Loan on North Street in Pittsfield. Joan and I will drop by later this afternoon to see if the key is one of theirs," I said.

"We have a slip of paper with numbers on it that was in a value added tax book in Peter Pickering's office. The numbers could be for bank accounts, telephones, or GPS coordinates. Who knows? Maybe it's a code. We'll make copies for you."

The meals were decent for a family restaurant, so we didn't need to contact the president of Friendly's for his money back guarantee promised on his TV advertisement. Because I ordered the baked haddock and chips, I didn't need to ask anyone to cut my food and get razzed about not being able to eat with one hand.

By the end of lunch, we had covered all the details of the case with the only interruptions coming when the waitress took the order, served the food, and refilled the coffee mugs. Since Janyce, Jerry, and Bill were helping out unofficially, I picked up the tab for everyone and left a generous tip.

Oddly enough, I just happened to remember we used to call this kind of unauthorized activity, a Swiss Navy Project because as a land-locked country, they don't have a navy.

Thanking everyone for their help, I shook hands with Jerry and Bill but gave Janyce a big hug with a kiss on the cheek. We returned to my car at the motel and took off for the Berkshire Bank in Pittsfield with Joan behind the wheel. I only had to remind her once to slow down once since we weren't in a hurry or in Washington, DC, traffic. I didn't want to sound like a broken record and have her start worrying too much about how sore I was.

After sitting down with the Berkshire Bank manager, we explained the key may relate to a Homeland Security case. Joan displayed her government identification and said we could obtain the necessary court orders, but asked if we could just find out what the key fits, if it was in fact one of theirs.

Examining the key carefully, he said it was one of theirs for a safe deposit box in their branch in Great Barrington, Massachusetts. He asked if we could obtain the owner's permission or if the owner could go there with us. We told him the owner was in a coma and his life may still be in danger. We informed him that the account may be in the name of Peter Pickering or the Three P Company based in Framingham.

He entered Peter's name on his computer and wrote down the account number for us. After he promised us that our conversation would be kept confidential, we thanked him for his help. We were assured that he would call the branch manager and ask her to cooperate with us fully.

With Joan behind the wheel, we made good time driving down to the Great Barrington branch and arrived well before closing time. As we entered the bank, a sweet young thing, who looked like she was all of twelve years old, politely said in a sing-song voice, "Good afternoon, how may I help you?"

I asked myself, *Is it possible that I am really getting that old?*

I said, "I'm Tom Powers," as Joan handed her a business card. "We're here to see Ms. Kathy McMillan. I believe she is expecting us."

"Certainly, sir," she replied. "Please follow me."

This caused Joan to elbow my good arm and whisper, "You got sired," followed by a wink and a chuckle she tried to suppress without much success.

"It was probably due to my natural, endearing charm," I whispered back, flashing her with one of my best smiles.

Having been lead into the manager's office, Joan produced her federal identification and the slip of paper with the account number handwritten under a Berkshire Bank letterhead. She said, "We just came from your main office in Pittsfield. I believe they were going to call ahead to advise we were on our way. We would like to open the safe deposit box for that account."

"Certainly, I have been expecting you. Please come right this way," Ms. McMillan said as she picked up a key from her desk top that appeared to be identical to the one we had and lead us to a large vault.

Once the safe deposit box was unlocked with the pair of keys, she said, "I'll leave you for now. Please push that button when you are finished, and I'll return."

Not knowing what to expect, Joan cautiously opened the box and peered inside. Removing a receipt with an account number from the Zurich location of the Union Bank of Switzerland (UBS AG), I dug into my pocket and verified the long number from the bookmark we found in Framingham matched the UBS account number. Inside there was also a key stamped with UBS. Removing both items and closing up the box, we signaled the manager to let her know that we were finished.

12

Returning to the motel, I called Alex and filled him in on everything we had uncovered up to this point. He was concerned about my shoulder wound and suggested I might want to take time off to recuperate. Alex said he could find someone else to help Joan out with the investigation in the meantime. I lied when I told him that the bullet only hit soft tissue and wasn't serious enough to slow me down. *Besides I could really use the work right now*, I told myself.

He was pleased that the news of discovering the safe deposit box in Switzerland could offer positive clues on the investigation since we didn't have much to go on yet. It was decided that our best course of action would be to go check out the UBS box in Zurich and contact all the customers in Switzerland from the Three P Company list supplied by Lucille to see if we couldn't retrace Peter's steps before he was attacked. Then we might be able to find out who tried to kill him and why.

There had been no obvious external improvement in Peter's condition, save his vital signs being more regular and his reflex movements seemed to be more frequent. Based on his brain function monitoring, the increases in EEG activity were taken as a positive sign he was improving.

Monique had not left his side for any length of time since we were there. At Alex's request, Sue Strelow, his administrative assistant, came over to obtain Monique's sizes and discuss her preferences in clothes and colors.

She later told Alex she was pleased with the selections Sue had picked out, but Alex surmised that Monique was more interested in Peter's welfare and medical progress than what she looked like. He said she was beginning to appear worn down from worrying so much about Peter.

Alex had arranged for a bed in the next room for her, but she rarely left Peter's side, even to eat. When she wasn't reading to him, Monique would just sit there, hold his hand, and talk to him for hours on end.

As I hung up after the extended phone call with Alex, Joan came back from her room and said, "We're all set for our direct flight from Newark, New Jersey, to Zurich on United Airlines tomorrow morning.

"Flying out of Albany, New York or Hartford, Connecticut would have added three to twelve hours trip time by heading south or west to get east after changing planes. We could get there from Boston, but we wouldn't be able to get home after without one or two very long stops.

"This way, the trip time would be only eight hours out on United and nine hours back on the Swiss Air return flight. I charged the e-tickets to your credit card so it would only be in your name—daddy."

"What did I tell you about all that sassy talk?" I said with a grin.

"Well, originally you were supposed to be looking after me. Now you are my unofficial dad as well, or at least until the case is finished."

"Speaking of your official dad, do you tell him when you will be outside of the country?"

"I used to, but he became such a busybody, I stopped keeping him informed where I was for the most part. He'd become such a worrywart I didn't know what else to do with him. What he doesn't know won't hurt him. Since we need to get an early start tomorrow, why don't you stay here and rest while I go fill your gas tank? I noticed that it was down to less than a quarter of a tank."

"I hate to say it, but that's probably a good idea. I am pretty sore. Thanks. I'll just lie here and watch the news while you're gone."

Not long after the world news had finished, there was a rap on the door. I started to get up when I realized it was the connecting door between our two rooms. Joan stuck her head through the doorway with her eyes closed, hand over her face, and said, "Are you decent?"

"No, but I'm reasonably proficient."

Joan entered my room carrying a large flat box and said, "There was a pizza shop next to the gas station. I didn't know what your preferences were, so I ordered a combination of everything except anchovies. You can pick off whatever toppings you don't care for. I grabbed a cold bottle of caffeine-free, diet Pepsi too."

"That sounds great. Thank you," I said while Joan found a couple of styrene cups in the bathroom, sealed in film wrappers.

"I brought back paper plates, napkins, and disposable utensils so we wouldn't have to clean up anything before we leave in the morning."

"Good thinking," I said as I slowly moved to the table in the kitchenette.

While we were eating, I noticed that NCIS followed the news on CBS. "It's too bad crimes aren't as easy to solve in the real world as the ones on TV," I said.

"Unless the programs are continued, they find the bad guys in less than an hour and take the rest of the week off. Maybe we should hire some of those people. They never seem to get shot either," Joan said with a smile.

"Those are just actors. The authors are the ones that know where and how to find the criminals. We should just hire the writers and ask them how to manage these cases. Good pizza by the way. Do you want that last slice?"

"No, I've had all I can handle. Go ahead and help yourself," she said as she started to pick up everything else on the table. "I left a wake-up call for us at 6:00 AM so we can get an early start. I hope you'll be feeling better tomorrow. It's a three-hour drive down to Newark if we don't hit any traffic jams. Good night, Tom."

"Good night, Joan. Thank you for all your help today," I said, glad to have her along as a partner after all.

13

Following a swing past the drive through window at Dunkin' Donuts in Lennox first thing in the morning, we were crossing the New York state line before my coffee was even cool enough to sip. After zipping further west a few miles on Interstate 90, we were headed south on the New York Thruway before I had time to finish eating my breakfast sandwich.

"We were in such a rush to check out of the motel this morning and get on the road, I didn't get a chance to ask you how you're feeling today," Joan said as she placed her coffee back into the cup holder and set the cruise control to just above the speed limit.

"My shoulder is still stiff, but not quite as sore as it was yesterday. Thank you for asking. When the pain subsides a little more, I should start doing a little physical therapy each day before it atrophies."

"Well, since you refused bed rest at the hospital, why don't you recline your seat back and try to get a little more sleep before we get to the airport? There's no guarantee we'll have a smooth ride on the plane or your shoulder won't get bumped if the seating in coach is crowded."

"I guess you're right, but I thought I was supposed to be looking out after you. Maybe you will make someone a good mother someday. Just don't get me any more speeding tickets. I already have acquired enough on my own as it is," I said as I put my head back and closed my eyes.

"Tom, wake up, we're at the airport in the *live parking only*, unloading zone. Slide over to the driver's seat while I check the luggage curbside. Then you can wait for me at the United Airlines ticket counter while I drop off your car in long-term parking."

"Boy, that was fast getting down to the Newark Airport from Massachusetts. I can't believe I still feel so tired and weak. It's like I have no energy at all."

"Losing as much blood as you did when you were shot will do that to you. I'll be right back."

"Okay, Tom, our baggage is checked through to Zurich. Slide out of the car, and I'll meet you inside at the ticket counter as soon as I find a place to park."

I wandered inside to find the kiosk to print out our e-tickets. It's hard to believe we had to pay this kind of money for tickets and then have to do the paper work processing for the airlines. Because I don't know how to type, it didn't really matter that I could only use one hand. Apparently hunt and peck typing isn't any faster with two hands.

"Oh, hi, Joan, there you are. Since my shoulder is still so sore, I requested handicap assistance to get to the gate. I didn't know if I'd have a problem walking that far. They need to see your photo identification and passport to check you in. Then we can wait over by the pay phones for a set of wheels and a pusher."

"We're going out on from Terminal A, but we'll be returning on Swiss Air to Terminal B. Did you have any problem finding a parking spot in the long-term lot?"

"No, I lucked out with a space that was being vacated in the second row just as I pulled up. That's probably your wheelchair assist coming toward us over there," Joan said as she waved her boarding pass over her head to attract his attention. "Do you think you're really up for this trip?"

"I'm still hurting a lot, but I should be doing better in a few days," I said, easing myself carefully into the wheelchair.

The only hassle we encountered in getting to the gate was when security insisted my sling be removed. There was also the fact that I couldn't raise my bum arm over my head when TSA asked me to for the photo imaging. At the gate, we didn't have to wait long for the announcement that those needing assistance or additional boarding time could go first. Once we were on board, we decided it would be best if we switched seat assignments so my left arm would be next to the window to prevent it from getting bumped.

After we settled in, I glanced over at Joan in the middle seat. Having been on my own for the last dozen years, nobody had paid attention to me like she has. I saw a perky, kind, capable, thoughtful, and intelligent woman who has everything going for her that any man could possibly want. That is, of course, working under the assumption one is looking for somebody to share their life with.

I must be getting delusional. Who said I was looking for anyone special? It didn't work for me the last time, and I'm way too old for Joan. I don't have anything to offer someone as nice as she is. She deserves so much more than what I could provide.

She turned and said with a gorgeous smile that lit up her whole face, "Are you comfortable?"

"I'm fine, don't keep worrying about me. I'll be doing better in a few days."

"Hey, you saved me from a bullet. I've got a vested interest if you're going to be responsible for me from now on."

"I have enough trouble being responsible for myself, let alone someone else. Even though your dad doesn't think so, it looks as though you are more than capable of taking care of yourself without any assistance or interference from him or me."

"Well, I owe you big time for pushing me out of the way of that bullet. Put this pillow behind your head, shut up, and get more rest."

"You forgot to say, or else," I said, smiling as the seat belt light went off so I could recline in my seat.

14

I awoke during our descent over the Alps shrouded in clouds. It felt strange that this was the first time I didn't feel totally exhausted since I was shot.

"And how does Rip Van Winkle feel today?" Joan asked, being her usual chipper self.

"I don't know about him, but I'm feeling much better now, thank you," I said. "I must have really needed the sleep. They say it takes much longer to heal when you get older."

"You look like you're in pretty good shape to me, except for that sling hanging around your neck," Joan said as the seat belt light came on.

I gritted my teeth and braced myself with my right arm against the seat in front of me in anticipation of the pain I thought was to follow, but the landing was surprisingly smooth.

Getting off the plane, the wheelchair I'd reserved in Newark was waiting for me at the top of the landing ramp. Always in a hurry, Joan was off and running toward baggage claim to find our luggage as soon as it hit the conveyor. By the time I arrived, she had just found our second piece. She grabbed both bags and followed me while I was still being pushed by the charming young woman who brought me there from the terminal gate.

With many people having a fear of flying, one would think that they'd avoid use of terms like terminal and depart. I'm certainly not ready for my departure and don't want to be a terminal case. Go figure.

As we rounded the corner to the customs area, we were greeted by a large room packed with at least a full plane load new arrivals, slowly snaking their way to the eight custom agents at the other side. Without saying a word, the woman pushing me unclipped the velvet barrier rope to allow us to pass through. We went directly around the perimeter of the crowd in the handicap aisle to the front of the long lines.

Following a precursory glance at our American passports, we found ourselves at the car rental counter in no time at all. I felt a little guilty about cutting past all the people waiting for a customs agent, but not so much.

I gave my wheelchair pusher a generous tip in US currency, said, "Thank you," and told her we'd be okay on our own from that point. I had reserved a Ford Focus at Hertz in my name so Joan wouldn't be listed as the lessee in the rental agreement. I added her as a driver though to keep the insurance intact in the event of an accident. At US $303 per week, the price was a bargain for an American four-door car with headroom.

I called the number Alex had given me at the Zurich Polizei Department and asked for Captain Johann Munzinger to inform him our plane was on time and we would meet him at the Union Bank of Switzerland (UBS) shortly.

When we arrived at the UBS and asked to see the branch manager, Captain Munzinger was already with him in his office. Joan presented her government credentials. We proceeded to explain that Peter Pickering was in the hospital and couldn't come in person. We asked for access to the box number on his receipt and requested the transaction be kept under the utmost secrecy because his life might still be in danger.

In the back of the vault, Captain Munzinger and the manager left us on our own once the safe deposit box was unlocked. Opening it up, we were pleasantly surprised that the first thing we found on the top was Peter's journal with the light blue cover.

A bundle of shipping documents with routing papers suggested he had copied all the pertinent package tracking information. That way the CIA could determine the ultimate destinations of his shipments to trading companies by checking the timing with ships leaving ports, railroad schedules, and trucking manifests.

Joan and I emptied the entire contents of the safe deposit box into the expandable valise I had brought along in the hopes of finding just such a potential bonanza of information.

After the box was locked and returned, we conveyed our appreciation to the UBS manager for his cooperation. On the way out of the Union Bank, we thanked Captain Munzinger profusely for his assistance. We also advised that we'd get back to him if we uncovered anything useful from what we found at the bank.

Once we were back in the rental car, I said, "Let's get to the hotel so we can take a look at the contents of the safe deposit box and figure out what our next move will be."

Joan punched the address into the GPS and said, "Well, it's not quite a hotel, Tom."

"What does that mean? Where will we be staying?" I asked.

"I started to check out the hotels in downtown Zurich and the least expensive ones would cost us three hundred to five hundred US dollars per night for two rooms in the city. Since we don't know if anyone else was aware of the UBS account, I figured we'd be better off outside the city while we're trying to figure out who we're up against. I booked us into Rheinfall Hostel in Neuhausen. It's sixteen miles from here."

"We're on an expense account. How much is that going to save?"

"It only costs fifty-four US dollars a night. I just thought nobody would think of looking for us there. It's rated at two stars."

"What do we get for fifty-four dollars at a hostel, Joan?"

"We get a bunk bed in a co-ed dorm, but we have to share a bathroom with others. I can take the top bunk so you won't mess up your shoulder though. It does have Internet access. We've both had worse when we were in the service. Are you afraid of a little roughing it?" Joan asked as she looked over at me with that dazzling smile of hers and sparkling eyes.

"Okay, we'll see how it works out."

Talk about tempting fate, I told myself. I thought I would be able to concentrate on the case with her in a separate room at night. Now we're going to share the same bunk bed. I'll have to keep reminding myself that I'm almost old enough to be her father.

15

The waterfall on the Rhine River at 450 feet wide with a vertical drop of 75 feet was an impressive sight as we drove by slowly. It is reportedly the biggest falls in the middle of the continent.

Once we were checked in at the Rheinfall Hostel, we had to figure out what we had obtained from the UBS safe deposit box in Zurich that might tell us what happened to Peter and why. Did he stumble upon too much information that the bad guys wanted to keep under wraps? Was he getting too close to finding out who was using American technology that might ultimately be employed by terrorists to attack Americans?

We decided that Joan would continue with the work Peter had initiated. Starting with the shipping documents from the Three P Company, she could cross reference them with schedules at ports, truck terminals, and railroad yards. The objective would be to try to determine the final destinations of the goods. I would begin with Peter's journal to see if I could tell who Peter met with on his last trip and who he dealt with on a frequent basis.

Beginning at the end of the journal entries, it appeared it had not been updated since his prior trip to Europe. Peter's last recorded visit was to see a Dutchman named Maarten van Rijn who did business from his office in Zurich, Switzerland, under the company name Mikrowelle AG. The notes indicated he could reduce his value added tax burden from the ongoing 78 percent rate in Holland to the 44 percent net tax he paid by doing business through his Swiss office.

He mostly shipped through the port of Bremen in Germany. According to the entries, the duties paid at this location were well below average for these commodities. Peter wrote in his log that he suspected it was probably because someone van Rijn knew or bribed would let the shipments slide through as a lower level of assembly or in a less-expensive product category.

Perhaps Peter had the book on value added taxes in his Framingham, Massachusetts, office to study trends. That way he could see how many others used this method to reduce their tax and duty bites.

Thumbing back through prior journal entries, it appeared that many of the sub-assemblies Peter was supplying to Mikrowelle were replacement components for Litton microwave-convection ovens from the United States. They had long lead times because these parts were for older models that had to be scheduled on special production runs.

The next to last entry was about Hans Zeigler of Dieckmann AG in Geneva. Almost all of his orders were for thermal/velocity sensors and optical/electromechanical switches. Again these items had long delivery times because they were no longer stock items in inventory. Many had been made obsolete by the newer digital technology.

Looking at earlier entries, I was surprised by the next previous item in sequence. The Lotus Trading Company in Taipei, Taiwan, returned a shipment of parts. It was routed through Hong Kong from the Korean People's Army Ground Force (KPAGF) at the North Korean Port of Chongjin.

According to Peter's notes, this was the first time anyone had tried to return a shipment originating from his firm. That made it possible for him to track the goods back to their final destination where the delivery was not accepted. Peter thought the delivery rejection was odd since the items specified on the purchase order were in complete agreement with the shipping manifest.

The attack on Peter could have been precipitated because the KPAGF realized that fact. He apparently had double-checked and found the components were ordered by the part number that was shipped after a dedicated production run of the obsolete item. It was hard to believe the North Koreans would order a hit on a supplier because KPAGF had screwed up by ordering the wrong part number.

Joan was still in the middle of trying to match shipment arrival dates from the Three P Company suppliers to possible destinations when I interrupted her. "Are you at a point when you can break loose for a few minutes? I want you to read this section of Peter's journal."

"Sure, what's up?" she said, marking her place in the stack of shipping invoices with a paper clip.

"Peter may have become a target because he found out where one of his orders was sent to. Obviously he didn't get a chance to tell the CIA before the bad guys got to him. While you're doing that, I'll call the American Embassy in Bern to have the CIA get weapons for us before the North Koreans find out we're involved. Until my shoulder heals, I'm in no shape to duke it out with anyone. From prior experience over here, I know it's not easy for nonresidents to purchase guns in either Switzerland or Germany."

"Oh, don't worry. I can protect you until you're back on your feet," she said with that mischievous grin of hers that tends to totally disarm me. "Then you can begin to fulfill your obligation of looking after me."

"Hey, let's get serious here. Remember what happened to Peter. For all we know, the same people who tried to do him in might know who and where we are," I said before I could start to contemplate what her taking care of me could entail.

"Okay, lighten up. I'm always on the alert for trouble," Joan replied as she returned her focus to the journal.

Joan was still reading the journal when I finished making arrangements to have the CIA meet us with a pair of handguns complete with holsters. "Now that we know Peter confirmed a link with North Korea, you probably should concentrate on the timing of shipments to the Lotus Trading Company and Hong Kong to see what ship and flight departures might match up with the North Korean Port of Chongjin as a destination," I said.

"I recently read that 24 percent of North Korea's four million US dollars worth of foreign trade is funneled through that port going to and coming from Hong Kong. Most of that consists of cars and electronic components.

"The North Koreans once had an ongoing business with places like Cuba, Syria, and Iran to fix their obsolete Russian weapons. Unfortunately for them, the repair quantities had fallen off due to shoddy workmanship by North Korea. Now they're trying to replace that business."

"Tom! Your shoulder is bleeding," Joan shouted as she rushed across the room.

I looked down, saw the dried blood, and said, "It must have been a slow leak. I don't think I hit anything, and it doesn't hurt any more than it did before."

"Here, let me get your shirt off to see what it looks like," Joan said as she unbuttoned the front, removed the sling, and carefully separated the bloody shirt from the dressing.

"Boy, talk about nimble fingers. I've never been able to unbutton a shirt that fast. Calm down. It's probably time to change the bandages anyway. I have fresh replacements just inside the top of my suitcase."

Joan gently peeled my shirt down to my waist like a banana. "It looks like it's just the entry wound in the front that's bleeding a little, the stitches seem to be holding okay," she said as she slowly removed the tape and bandage from the wound. "I'll go see if I can round up a small basin and washcloth to clean that up."

Joan soon returned with a pair of small rectangular plastic tubs filled with soapy water stacked at a right angle to each other and a couple of clean washcloths. "We're going to have to restrict your activity for a couple of days while that heals," she said as she proceeded to dab the front wound with a damp cloth.

After completing the same procedure on the back of my shoulder, she dried both areas with the other clean cloth and applied antibiotic ointment on fresh dressings to both sides. "Stand up slowly and drop your trousers," she said more as an order than a request.

Surprised, I said, "What?"

"You heard me. We can't have you bending and stretching for a few days if the sutures are going to do their job. I might as well give you a sponge bath while I'm all set up for it. That's why I brought the extra tub."

I reluctantly complied, even though I was experiencing difficulty in suppressing my normal masculine urges with her being this close while she tended to the wounds. My printed boxer shorts might help to conceal the state of arousal evidence better than tighty whities, but not by much.

I tried to ignore the lightness of her touch and the warmth of her breath on my bare skin without much success. Joan's attention directed at me with the fluttering cloth felt like I was being overpowered by the herd of butterflies in my stomach. If she was uncomfortable with the situation, she kept it well hidden and seemed to be all business by concentrating on the task at hand.

Before she finished with my upper torso, I tried to remember who won the Super Bowl last year and what the final score was, but I was blanking. All I could think of was that I was alone with this gorgeous creature who seemed to be attracted to me for some strange reason, which totally defied logic.

Not knowing anything about what her dad looked like, I conjured up the image of a huge, angry man chasing me away from his precious daughter. That seemed to help suppress the natural reaction that would have caused substantial embarrassment, at least on my part.

Finishing up on my legs, she stood facing me as she replaced my sling and said, "There, you can take care of the rest. Doesn't that feel much better?"

It took every bit of fortitude I could muster up to not wrap my good arm around her and pull her close to me. "Yes, thank you, but you didn't have to do all that."

"Yes, I did if we are going to get you back on your feet enough so you can help me on this case. An infection could result in a major setback. Besides, you need to be fully functional if you are going to be responsible for me," she said as she grinned and playfully tapped me on the side of my chin with her open palm.

I tried not to react to her touch, once again reminding myself, *You are too old for her, and she deserves better than what you have to offer.* I replaced the first aid supplies in my suitcase and extracted a clean set of clothes.

Gathering up an armful of clothes from her luggage and stacking them on the table where she was working, Joan announced, "I'm going to go take a quick shower myself while you change up."

16

I was adjusting my sling after I finished dressing when Joan returned from the shower wrapped in a bath towel with her hair wound up in another. "Ta-da," she announced as she entered our room and headed for the folding Japanese dressing screen in the corner. The silk fabric stretched over the black enamel lacquered frame had been hand painted with peacocks and flowers. While it looked attractive and fairly expensive, it seemed to be out of place in this setting. "Here I am all bright, shiny, and clean again. Are you half as hungry as I am?"

"Actually I'm starving. I slept through the meal on the plane. Did you have a place to eat in mind?"

"Well, this area is part of the German section of Switzerland. It so happens I noticed a little place a few miles back on the way here called Schnitzelhuus. The sign out front said German cuisine. It kind of looked like an old-fashioned European-style neighborhood restaurant. Do you want to give it a try?" she asked as she flipped the towels up over the screen and successively grabbed items of her clothing one at a time from the other side of the screen top.

"That sounds good as long as I have a choice of something other than German sausage. Some of them don't agree with my stomach," I said as she stepped out from behind the screen looking absolutely ravishing. "I thought you said you didn't have much of a wardrobe. You look fantastic in that outfit."

"Thank you. It's one of the two dressy combinations I own. With the extra jacket and coordinating slacks, I can mix and match when I travel. There's a local telephone directory up on the shelf. I'll see if I can find a listing for the restaurant. We'll probably need reservations."

Looking through the phone book she asked, "Do you think this skirt is too short?

"Well, I'm no expert, but I'm also in no condition to help you fight off all the young guys you're going to be attracting tonight."

"Tom! I thought I left my father back at home in the States. You're supposed to be my partner. Whoops, it's ringing," she said as she held up one finger. "Hello." Covering the speaker on her phone, she added, "I think they said they would get someone that speaks English."

When Joan hung up, she said they were booked solid, but just had a cancellation and could squeeze us in if we got there soon.

I said, "If they're that busy with local patrons, the food is probably pretty good."

We were immediately seated upon our arrival. The place was small with a limited number of tables, so it felt both cozy and charming. The rustic walls were adorned with pictures of European royalty. The service people in their traditional German clothing were quick, attentive, and friendly. The large portions of schnitzel were served hot, and the chips were fresh and crispy.

On the way out, I said, "Joan, that was fantastic, but if I had one more stein of ale, you would have had to carry me out of there."

"Yeah, I'm stuffed too. It was a nice change of pace from fast food though."

After the delightful conversation we shared over a wonderful dinner, we were lost in our own thoughts on the ride back to the hostel. Even though our time together was brief, it seemed we had known each other forever.

"You know I'm kind of bushed. Why don't we get a good night's rest and tackle the journal and shipment invoices again after we pick up our weapons at the American Embassy in Bern tomorrow morning?"

"That sounds like a plan," Joan said as she pulled into the parking lot.

Back in the room, Joan ducked behind the screen and placed her clothes neatly on top as she changed into her robe. "Is there anything I can get for you before I turn in?"

"No, I'm all set. Thank you for all your help today. I'll get the light. Good night, Joan, pleasant dreams."

As I watched her nimbly climb the ladder to the top bunk, I wondered, *Why couldn't I find someone like her closer to my own age?* Then I flipped the switch.

To rub that very point in my face, a sweet "Good night, Daddy" rained down like a cold shower from the bunk above.

17

I woke to a bright ray of sunshine in my face and looked at the clock. It said 6:00 AM. How could that be? I checked my watch. It said midnight, real time to civilized folk back in the Eastern Daylight Time Zone. Darn jet lag anyway.

Blinking a few times to clear my vision and shaking my head to loosen the cobwebs, I rolled over to see Joan busy in the kitchenette. She was fully dressed, sporting the patented grin that only she could wear and do it justice. She was humming softly as she set two steaming hot cups of black coffee on the table next to the two pairs of granola energy bars.

"Where did you manage to find the coffee?" I asked.

"I keep a small plastic jar of instant coffee in my luggage with a few snacks."

"Of course you do. When you told me you were a tomboy, I didn't realize you were a Boy Scout as well. What is their motto again? Oh, that's it, be prepared. If you can cheer down long enough for me to take a few sips, perhaps I can wake up enough to participate in a meaningful conversation."

"Please pardon the observation, but you still look horrible. At least there are no outward indications that your shoulder has started to bleed again, but you might want to change into something cooler. It's supposed to be uncomfortably hot today."

Looking down, I realized that I was still so tired last night that I went to sleep in my clothes, which were now abysmally wrinkled.

The granola bars were exceptionally dry. "Exactly how old is this health food you've been lugging around anyway?"

"I have no idea. I just replenish the supply when it runs low," she said.

"Actually they are not too bad when washed down with enough coffee," I said. "Thank you for sharing your stash."

Soon after we finished our snack, we were on the way to the American Embassy in Bern. Except for a few farmers driving their tractors and horses between fields, we didn't encounter much in the way of traffic that would slow us down.

I had to marvel at Joan's self-sufficiency and ability to multitask. It seemed she never needed to ask for help. After punching in the embassy street address, she would glance over at the GPS occasionally to check on the next turn without interrupting the flow of our conversations.

All of a sudden Joan paused in mid-sentence and said, "There's a silver Audi that's been lagging behind us for a couple of miles, even with plenty of opportunities to pass. It may be nothing, but I'm going to try to lose it just in case. I'll feel better once we have weapons for protection again."

With that said, she gradually accelerated to ten kilometers per hour faster. Once we had achieved about a half mile of separation, she executed a ninety-degree turn behind a tree after going around a curve and then slammed on the brakes. "Quick, duck down so they can't see us."

"How am I supposed to do that with my sore shoulder?"

"I'll lie on the seat and you lean over me with your left arm hanging to the floor. Quick, hurry up!"

We had gained enough time to get into position and be out of their line of sight before the Audi rounded the curve. After the car went past us and continued down the road, I found myself in an awkward position with my right hand resting on her butt and my left arm leaning against her warm, ample breasts.

Not being able to get any leverage by pulling myself up with my right hand on the steering wheel, I tried to grab the headrest on her seat. That didn't work either. "Joan, I've fallen, and I can't get up," I said as I started laughing, because I felt just plain silly to be in this predicament.

Since I was lying on top of her right arm and her left arm was under her, she was having trouble freeing up herself to push me off, so she started to giggle too. "This is ridiculous.

It shouldn't be all this hard. I'm afraid that I might jar your shoulder and start the bleeding again if I try to slide out from under you."

"Wait, let me try again," I said as I managed to slowly push myself up with my hand on her thigh. I was amazed that her leg muscles were so firm that they didn't seem to give at all. That little bit of elevation on my part was enough that she could extract her right arm and help push me up the rest of the way up without bumping my left arm.

Once we were both sitting upright again, she simply asked, "Is your shoulder okay?"

"My shoulder is fine. I'm sorry if I put you in an uncomfortable situation though. I didn't mean to pin you in a wrestling hold."

"Don't worry about it. I've been out on dates that were harder to get off me," she said with a grin. "It looks as if that silver Audi is long gone. Maybe it was a false alarm, but it's better to err on the side of caution. We can watch to see if it shows up again."

As she made a U-turn and pulled back on the main road, I wondered for a moment exactly what she was thinking when we were that close together. She's becoming far too difficult for me to resist. If she is half as attracted to me as I am to her, I'm in big trouble, and we'll never be able to solve this case together.

The central part of Bern was a medieval city on a hilly peninsula surrounded on three sides by the Aare River, situated in the German section of Switzerland. As we approached the city driving through the leafy hills, we still hadn't spotted the Audi again.

We entered the embassy just in time for our meeting and were immediately ushered into Barbara Beyer's office. I was surprised that the U S ambassador to Switzerland and Liechtenstein bore such a striking resemblance to Jamie Lee Curtis. She seemed to be fairly young for such a political plum assignment, but maybe what she lacked in experience she made up for in youthful energy.

We asked if she could arrange to have two copies of Peter's journal and the invoices from his UBS safe deposit box made. One set would be dispatched to Alex and the other copies would be given to the resident CIA agents in Switzerland. After she asked an administrative assistant to make the duplicates, agents Alma MacIntosh and Rob Ford were ushered into her office.

Alma had flaming red, naturally curly Celtic hair with an excess of freckles and intense green eyes. She displayed her dimples when she offered a courteous smile but shook my hand with a firm grip that felt like she had spent her youth milking cows every morning. Underneath the friendly exterior demeanor, a hidden undercurrent suggested she was not to be trifled with.

Rob seemed to be the more transparent and amicable of the two with a jovial manner. At six-foot-four or five, he could pass for a poster child of a Scandinavian athlete with the broad shoulders of a lumberjack, light blond hair, and deep blue eyes.

Following introductions, Rob handed us a briefcase with weapons, holsters, and ammunition. Alex had instructed them to provide any assistance we needed, so contact information and untraceable burner phones were included in the case as well.

We were told that Peter Pickering had regained consciousness, but still had a full-blown case of amnesia. Physically it appeared he was finally out of the woods, but time would be required to see how fast his memory returns, if ever. At the conclusion of the meeting, we headed back to our hostel.

18

We grabbed a quick bite to eat, a number of snacks, and a few grocery items on the return trip to the hostel. There didn't appear to be anyone following us this time, so the people on our tail in the Audi on the trip out to Bern probably had no interest in what we were doing. At least I felt more secure now that I had a side arm for protection.

With Joan driving, I had time to think about Peter's many journal entries that involved the Dutchman named Maarten van Rijn and his Mikrowelle AG Company in Switzerland. The high frequency of the entries suggested he might be either one of Peter's major customers or someone who clamors for attention. I thought that perhaps we should see if there was a way to connect him with the return shipment from North Korea via Hong Kong and Taiwan.

When we got back to Rheinfall, Joan resumed digging through the pile of customer invoices. Sure enough, she found the return authorization order from Taipei, Taiwan, that was required to ship it back to Mikrowelle AG in Zurich.

Perhaps it was no coincidence that Peter's safe deposit box was located at the Zurich branch of the United Bank of Switzerland. It is possible that he was in Zurich on business often enough for it to be a convenient location for him. I figured we should see if we can learn anything about Peter's disappearance at Mikrowelle. Rather than warn them in advance that we were coming to talk to them, we decided we would drop by unannounced early the next day.

I turned to Joan and said, "I hate to admit it, but I feel downright tuckered out."

"Well, it's little wonder considering what you've been through. The hospital didn't give you any transfusions, so it will take a while for your body to build up your blood supply again. After the trip to get here and bouncing over the back roads today, you are hardly keeping your promise to follow the doctor's orders and rest.

"If they had their way back at the hospital, you'd still be camped out in your semiprivate room. Then you'd be woken in the middle of the night for pain pills and sucking on Jell-O in your little Johnny with your cute butt hanging out."

"I'll thank you to leave my butt out of this conversation, Ms. Walters."

"Hey, you can't blame me for noticing."

"For different reasons, I have to agree with your dad that we shouldn't start anything between us. Intimate relationships with a partner never work out. Besides, I'm too old for you anyway. You might want to settle down some day and start a family of your own. I've been there and done that. I wasn't good at being a husband, dad, and a police officer at the same time. I missed all the kids' school activities and sporting events."

"I'm sure that was because of your duties as a detective. Their jobs never end. I wouldn't want to go through everything my dad put up with from me when he was trying to raise me as a single parent. I made up my mind long ago that I don't want to be a mother."

"Hypothetically speaking, if we were to get serious and I were to retire around age sixty-five, you'd probably still be working for at least another ten or twenty years. What kind of relationship would that be for either of us anyway?"

"I'm only saying, nobody's got a crystal ball. There are no guarantees in life. I'm tired of wrestling matches with guys my age who haven't grown up yet. We both know what they're after. All they're looking for is a roll in the hay. They are way too immature for my taste and not the kind of people I would want to share my life with. At least you and I seem to see things the same way and can agree on an approach about how to do most things so far."

"You've just described why we probably will make good partners on the job. You're a talented young woman with a lot to offer a special young man down the road. You'll know it when you find him. In the meantime, age aside, you deserve a lot more than what I've got to offer."

"Now just wait a darn minute here, mister. One father is more than enough for me. I'll be the one to decide what I do on my own time and who I do it with. I don't need any advice on that score from my partner either. I will be solely responsible for the determination of what I think you might have to offer."

"Hey, Joan, I'm sorry if we got off on the wrong foot in this discussion. I thought we should establish some ground rules so we could concentrate on the case without distractions or complications."

"Yeah, you're probably right. There's no point in creating problems that don't exist anyway. I'll enter the address of the Dutchman's Zurich office in the GPS so it'll be all set in the morning when we're ready to leave. Then I can finally hit the sack. It's been a long day for me too."

Waiting for Joan to get up the steps to her upper bunk before I hit the light switch, I turned to see her effortless ascent of the ladder with her smooth, catlike movements. I couldn't help but notice how perfectly proportioned the outline of her body was as accentuated by the backlighting through her thin nightgown. Trying not to stare for too long, I flipped off the light as soon as she was settled in.

Someone once said that a dirty mind is a joy forever. I don't know if that is true, but I felt like a dirty old man every time my thoughts strayed to the possibility of any sort of a romantic relationship with Joan because of our age difference. I started to wonder exactly how much younger could a woman be who would be appropriate for me to consider dating?

The other issue is, how could we possibly work together effectively if we were personally involved on any level? How many times have I seen that create problems between mixed gender partners on the police squad? We don't need those kinds of headaches when we have to be on our toes out in the field.

What am I thinking about? I haven't even been out on a date in years. Who said I was interested in starting up a new relationship anyway? I have to put all this nonsense out of my mind if I'm ever going to get to sleep.

19

I woke to the mixed aroma of coffee, toast, and scrambled eggs. Adjusting my arm in the sling, I rolled out of bed to see Joan in front of the stove beaming her gorgeous smile in my direction. Standing there, looking so lovely in her gossamer thin gown, I wondered for a nanosecond if it would be appropriate for me to ask her to start wearing a robe when I'm around.

After all, how much temptation could a grown man withstand before I took her in my arms and did something we'd both regret? Well, wait a minute, since I only have one usable arm, maybe she'd be perfectly safe anyway. She certainly wouldn't have any problem resisting any unwanted advances from me.

Wiping out those thoughts that flashed through my brain, I just said, "Good morning, Joan. Thank you for taking care of breakfast two days in a row, but I'm not a total invalid, you know. I could take my share of turns. It all looks great and smells delicious by the way."

"That's okay. I've started to compose a ledger. Eventually I'm going to make certain the score gets evened up in the final accounting. When you regain the full use of your shoulder, you're going to owe me big time," she said with a chuckle. "Now sit down and eat before it gets cold."

"You've outdone yourself again. The eggs are light and fluffy. I half expected you to burn the toast, since you appear to be so good at everything else."

Once we were on the road back to Zurich, I looked over to watch Joan while she was driving. Except for having a lead foot on the accelerator, she did exceptionally well at that too.

As we pulled up to the curb at the address we were looking for in Zurich, we heard a muffled bang, even with the windows closed. Drawing our weapons, we ran to either side of the front door and cautiously peered inside. Not seeing anyone, Joan pointed to herself and quickly slipped inside the door before I could object. She keeps doing that.

We scanned the room and found no one in sight. Joan had her back to the wall next to the inner office door. This time, I went in first and fired two rounds at the chest of the short Asian guy pointing his gun at me from across the room. Joan knocked me down and rolled to the floor to kick the gun out of the hand of the woman aiming at me from a crouched position.

The young woman popped up to her feet and assumed a defensive martial arts stance, but Joan spun like a top to knock the legs out from under her. Before I could react, Joan had her in a full Nelson and said, "If you're not too busy, could you please put the nylon cuffs on her wrists?"

"Wow, where did you learn those moves?" I asked as I put the handcuffs on her would be attacker.

"I was on the men's wrestling team in college. Being a black belt, I was also good at hand-to-hand combat in the service," she said.

I went to check on her partner, but he had no pulse. That's when I noticed the guy on the floor behind the desk with a large caliber bullet hole in the middle of his forehead. Working under the assumption that he was the Dutchman, we dragged our captive out to the car before the local Swiss police showed up to ask too many questions we couldn't or didn't want to answer.

Joan sat in the back seat with our prisoner, and I proceeded to drive the standard shift with one arm in a sling. The rental car did an admiral job in the city, even with me skipping gears from first to third to minimize the amount of shifting I had to do in the heavy traffic.

Once we were out in the country again, driving wasn't as difficult. After she contacted the CIA agents we had met in Bern, Joan arranged for us to meet them back at the American Embassy.

Joan then turned her attention to our captive. Apparently she spoke enough English to find out her name is Kang Sang-hee. The name of her senior partner was Park Min-ho. They were on a special mission together from North Korea for their *Dear Leader*.

She said she was ashamed she couldn't reach her cyanide capsule with the handcuffs on. Sang-hee was worried that if she talked, they would kill everyone in her family being held captive in a labor concentration camp.

Before long, we were back on the American embassy grounds. Agents Alma MacIntosh and Rob Ford confirmed that the Dutchman, Maarten van Rijn, was the other body found at the Zurich office of Mikrowelle. After a thorough debriefing by Rob and Alma of everything that happened on this trip to Zurich, I traded the gun I fired at the older Korean spy for a replacement that couldn't be traced.

Once again we were on the way back to the hostel with Joan behind the wheel.

"I hope I didn't hurt you when I knocked you down in Zurich," she said.

"No I'm fine, thanks to you. Thank you for saving my life. That makes us even now. Your dad will be pleased to learn that you are no longer my responsibility."

"You say that like it's a good thing. Does that mean you don't want to be responsible for me anymore?" she said, grinning.

"I got the distinct impression from you that your father would blow a proverbial gasket if he ever found out we were anything other than partners."

"I don't understand why you are so anxious to get out of being responsible for me after you saved my life. I kind of liked having someone other than my dad looking after me for a change. Maybe the score isn't just even, and we haven't erased all of our obligations. Perhaps we now have to be responsible for each other."

"Joan, we talked about this. Anything more than us being partners on assignments can never work out between us. I'm too old for you. You deserve to find someone your own age with common interests to share your life with."

"Tom, I told you that one father is more than I need to give me advice. I'm old enough to decide what and who I want in my life."

As we pulled into the parking lot, Joan said, "We need to change the dressings on your wounds and let you get some rest. Then we can discuss where we're at on this assignment and what the next logical step would be."

Entering the room, Joan removed her gun and holster. Then she did the same with mine before lifting the sling over my head. Deftly, she unbuttoned and took off my shirt. She reached up to put her arms around my neck as she pressed against me. "Joan, that's probably not a good idea," I said.

"Don't you find me attractive?"

"That's the trouble. I find you almost impossible to resist."

"Then be quiet and kiss me."

I started to protest further when she covered my mouth with her warm, moist lips. Her arms dropped as she unfastened my belt and pants. Quickly she unbuttoned her blouse and let it fall to the floor. All the while she was holding the most wonderful kiss with her tongue exploring my mouth. I hadn't felt a connection like this with anyone in far too many years.

Breaking our lip lock, I said, "Joan, we can't do this. There'll be no going back to the way things were between us as partners."

"Who said I want to?" she said, unsnapping her bra and stepping out of her pants before she took my right arm and gently pulled me with her down to the rug.

"It won't work, I'm still too sore to move."

"I'll take care of all the action. Just lay back, relax, and enjoy us," she said while nibbling on my neck.

I was amazed with the fullness of her breasts and near-perfect proportions of her body. She must have had more sun exposure than I'd noticed since her face and neck were slightly darker than the rest of her body. For some strange reason, I found the contrast with the paleness of my skin next to hers very exciting. Then again, everything about her felt intoxicating, especially as she carefully rolled me on my back before climbing on top.

"Joan, are you absolutely certain you want to do this?" I said, hoping her answer would be affirmative.

"You sure waste a lot of time talking. Kiss me," she demanded as she slid all the way down and lowered her firm breasts to make contact with my chest. "Tell me if it hurts your shoulder at all."

Not waiting for an answer, she once again covered my mouth with hers as we jointly explored with our tongues. Her physique was phenomenal. Holding herself above me, she maintained full contact without adding noticeable weight to my upper body.

Her well-toned, coiled muscles were akin to those of a jungle cat ready to spring, but her movements were so soft, warm, and tender. She rocked back and forth like a spring breeze caressing the tree tops at the end of a storm. She was barely touching me but took firm control of every fiber of my being.

Leaning back to achieve deeper penetration, she drove me to distraction with a smooth circular motion of her hips as she massaged my stomach with her long, sensuous fingers. Achieving an orgasm just before I did, she slowly lowered her whole body over mine.

In a very soft, sultry voice she said, "Do you suppose this is what Alex had in mind when he asked us to work closely together?"

"I'm sure it was the farthest thing from his mind. I know it was from mine."

Lifting herself slightly to take her weight off my chest, she asked, "How is your shoulder doing?"

"What shoulder?" I asked. "You had me and all my senses fully discombobulated fifteen minutes ago. Just make sure you put all my parts back where you found them when you're done."

"After all that protesting before on why we shouldn't be involved like this, do you still have any regrets now?" she said with an adorable smile.

"Only that we didn't meet years ago."

"It was good for me too, but you need to get some rest to heal and get your strength back. Then you can be a full participant one of these days soon. Let me help you up to your bunk so you can take a nap. If you don't mind being crowded, I can join you."

"I thought that is exactly what you just did," I said as we snuggled together on top of the sheet, sharing the single pillow. As she cuddled even closer, I closed my eyes and drifted off on a light, fluffy cloud not visited by me in a recent lifetime.

20

"Hey, dreamboat, I wondered when you were going to wake up from your nap."

"Whoa, how long was I out for?" I said, surprised it was already dark outside.

"A couple of hours. I thought you needed the rest, so I showered and made us a couple of sandwiches in the meantime. First I figured that you should have another sponge bath and your bandages changed. We can't take a chance on you having an infection. Come over and sit in this chair so we can attend to your wounds first."

Looking down, I realized that I didn't dream what had happened between us earlier. "Did the clothes fairy strip me naked while I was asleep?"

"Yes, I did. I thoroughly enjoyed taking advantage of you in your weakened condition. Not only that, I reveled in every minute of it," she said, smiling broadly.

"You were absolutely phenomenal. It seems hard to imagine something that wonderful could actually happen like that between us."

"Oh, it was hard all right. I'm sure you couldn't have derived more pleasure from our initial encounter than I did though. I hope you aren't sorry it finally happened. We owe each other our lives so we might as well take advantage of the fact that we survived," she said.

"Thank you for taking down the would be shooter today, by the way. Another bullet hole could have ruined my whole day. We are going to have to be more careful when we are out in the field from now on. We might not be so lucky the next time."

"That we're both still around to talk about it should be cause for celebration."

"If that was your idea of a celebration, I have no idea what you'd do for an encore to top that. I don't know where we can go from this point either," I said.

"Why do you worry so much about what's going to happen next? All this time I've been wondering why you were holding back. Did you want the same thing to happen between us as I did or not?"

"Yes, very much so, but it just didn't seem like it was the right thing for me to do. I felt that I would be messing up your life when I'm supposed to be looking after you."

"Tom, that's so sweet of you to say, but I'm a big girl. None of the guys I've dated have ever put my welfare or pleasure ahead of theirs. Think about it for a minute. At my age, you were married and had two kids. You figured out what you wanted to do on your own without the least bit of advice from anyone else.

"Up to this point, I've been dedicated to my career and didn't have time for family life or finding a compatible mate. It's up to me to figure out what's right for me and when that's going to happen. Nobody else can decide for me. Not you, and certainly not my father."

"Your dad is concerned about the difficulties you'd face as part of a mixed-race couple, Joan. It would seem that society's acceptance of racial equality has changed enough so that wouldn't be a problem for most people to deal with. I think the burdens imposed by adding our age difference on top of that would not be fair to you, however."

"So far, I like what I've seen about our possibilities and options in the future for the two of us. From where I stand, the benefits of us being a couple outweigh the drawbacks by far. Are you at least open to exploring the potential of teaming up together outside of our assignments or not?"

"For me it could be very exciting, but I hope that you won't be disappointed and regret your decision down the road."

"Just so you know, I think you are fantastic, and I'd like to see where this leads. So get your butt over here. I'll put fresh dressings on your wounds and give you that bath. If you don't behave yourself, I'll do it with my tongue instead of using a sponge."

"Yes, ma'am, right away," I said while saluting.

"Let's see what it looks like under the bandages. Ah, not too bad. Both the entry and exit wounds appear to be healing up quite nicely."

"You know for someone who is trained in the use of deadly force, you sure can be very gentle," I said, feeling drawn to her both because of the tenderness and the excitement generated by her touch.

"When we get you all healed up, we can try to see if you would prefer to be treated roughly," she said with a wink and a smile. "Stand up now so I can finish your bath. You know it is a lot easier to bathe you when you don't have clothes in the way. Maybe I can convince you to hang around naked all the time.

"In a few more days, I can remove the stitches. Then you can take a shower all by yourself, but where would be the fun in that?"

With Joan this close and touching me all over, it was all I could do to concentrate on other things and restrain myself.

"You know we're going to have to contact Alma and Rob first thing tomorrow morning to see if they learned anything from the Zurich police and Sang-hee.

"If North Korea had a contract out on the Dutchman, we might be getting close to finding out if there is anything else they are trying to cover up. Maybe once the police finish up at the Mikrowelle office in Zurich, we can get a look at their files."

"That sounds like a great idea, Tom, but I'm starting to get one of my own."

"And what would that be?"

"After we have something to eat, we could resume where we left off before your nap."

"While that would be very tempting, as the voice of reason, I should point out we have to figure out how we can manage to make any progress on the case. We should focus better and try to avoid personal interactions."

Dropping her robe to the floor, Joan put her arms around me, looked up, and said in a sultry voice, "How do we know for certain that would be detrimental to our work on our case unless we tried it at least once again to see if it is? Make sure you keep those fresh dressings clean," she said as she took my hand, led me to the lower bunk, proceeded to kneel down next to me, and kiss me all over.

"Joan, you're driving me up a tree."

"Well, maybe I'm doing it wrong, let's try something different to find out if you like it better. We have to make sure this won't cause a problem when we team up on future missions," she said as she mounted me again. "See if you can hold off for a while so we can really determine if we're doing it correctly."

The best I could tell, I somehow managed to last long enough for her to climax three times before I did.

"Wow, you were absolutely right. It is really going to be a problem trying to concentrate on business if we are distracted like that," she said as she rolled off to my side.

"That was unbelievable, but I don't understand why I'm totally spent when you did all the work."

"That's because you were instructed to get plenty of bed rest. So far we got you into the bed. Are you resting yet?" she asked with her lovely smile beaming.

"Joan, I don't know what to say. It will be some time before I can unwind and relax enough to contemplate resting. You are positively fantastic. I don't think I could ever say no to you."

"Good, then I have you right where I want you to be," she said, snuggling up on my good shoulder and sharing an extended kiss. "How was that for an encore, by the way?"

"If anyone had told me it could have been better the second time, there's no way I would have believed it. You sure know how to raise the bar and my emotions to new heights. Now I feel totally drained and sapped of energy. Are you comfortable being in that position?"

"I have never felt this good before. I didn't intend to wear you out when you should be recuperating. Just put your arm around me and close your eyes so we can get some sleep. Good night, Tom."

"Joan, just saying good night doesn't seem to cut it. You were everything I could have asked for today as a partner and tonight and a lover. Thank you for being you," I said as we cuddled a little closer.

21

As Joan slowly opened her eyes, she came to the realization that I was watching her. "Hey, babe, didn't anyone ever tell you that it is impolite to stare?" she said while gently pulling me toward her. She proceeded to give me a big hug and a long, passionate kiss.

"It's been forever since I've had anyone even half as gorgeous as you are to look at. You are simply the personification of charm, grace, and beauty."

"I'll bet that's what you say to all your partners you end up naked with while sharing a twin-sized bunk bed in a Swiss hostel."

"It's never happened to me before. Scout's honor," I said, holding up three fingers. "I'm kind of like a virgin in that regard. Is this where I mention that I've never been in a

Swiss hostel before? Perhaps that could that be a little secret between us?"

"You know that every last one of your secrets is safe with me. If you can roll off the bed, we can get dressed, and I can make coffee. Then we could have the sandwiches for breakfast we were going to eat for dinner last night. That was before we were sidetracked by some activity or other we ended wrapped up in."

"Since your coffee tastes a lot better than what I can make, I'll see if I might be able to reach Rob to find out what they learned from the police and Sang-hee."

"Maybe I should take a turn getting shot one of these days. You keep using the same lame excuse that you have trouble performing menial tasks with one arm. That sounds like an obvious cop out to me, if you'll pardon the expression."

"Well, you really didn't have any performance problems last night, and I certainly wouldn't classify your actions as menial. You had my complete and undivided attention. I found you nothing short of positively superb. You certainly didn't need any excuses and don't have to apologize for anything," I said, pulling her up close with my good arm for an endearing smooch.

After leaving a message for Rob, I got through to Alma. She said Kang Sang-hee decided to cooperate fully with the CIA. She would tell them everything she knew if they gave her a new identity. Apparently she claimed to have been on another assignment before rejoining Park Min-ho in

Switzerland. He was in Europe for some time, but she didn't know anything about his activities before she arrived.

Sang-hee said she knew nothing about Peter Pickering or the Three P Company. Her orders were to assist Park in taking out van Rijn. They were also supposed to destroy all his hard copy files and computer data in the office. Sang-hee had no idea why they were doing it. She had learned at a young and tender age not to question orders from her superiors.

It seems that the CIA convinced the police in Zurich to tell the news reporters that Maarten van Rijn and two unidentified Asians died in an apparent shoot out at Mikrowelle.

If the North Koreans believed Sang-hee had perished, her family members in custody could be out of danger. Because they were no longer useful as leverage against Snag-hee, they might even be released from captivity.

Joan had a steaming hot cup of coffee waiting for me when I finished my phone conversation with Alma.

I explained everything I had learned from Alma in between nibbling on my sandwich and sipping the coffee. It felt so good to get something into my stomach. I was running on empty.

Part of the assignment for the Korean spies was to destroy the files. That suggested there was information included in the office that could be useful to us.

If the deaths at Mikrowelle were handled by the CIA working with Interpol, the Zurich police wouldn't be contaminating the evidence by blindly sifting through the paper and computer files.

Rob and Alma planned to send in a moving crew to extract all the office furniture and computers to determine what could be learned at a location remote from the crime scene. We were to meet them the next day where they had rented a place for us to work on the second floor of an old office building located on the outskirts of Zurich.

Joan soaked all this in and said, "You realize what that means, don't you?"

"I have no idea what you think it means. Please enlighten me," I said, scratching my head.

"We can take the rest of the day off, and you can get some serious rest so you can be back on your feet again, sooner than later."

"Why do I think you have an ulterior motive here?"

"According to the ancient Chinese legend I quoted to you before, since I saved your life yesterday, I'm responsible for you now. I'm going to make sure you stay in bed and rest, even if I have to sit on top of you all day long."

"I thought you were doing that last night, and we both know how that turned out. I'm reasonably certain that's not what Dr. Broz meant by bed rest. You'll wear us both out if you don't slow the pace down a notch or two."

"I felt we had an ideal system established that was completely functional. I was being responsible for you and did all the work while you just rested. When you heal enough, you can take over. Then you will be responsible for me and do all the moving. See how fantastic that will be when you get a chance to even the score?"

"This is exactly what I was talking about yesterday, Joan. As wonderful as everything was between us last night, how are we ever going to concentrate on the task at hand when we are working together?"

"Do I detect an unsatisfied customer? I haven't enjoyed being with anyone else this much in my whole life. Perhaps I was being too selective. Maybe I was exercising too much restraint and self-denial, but I find being with you totally exhilarating. On the other hand, it might be because we are so much alike in many ways."

"I can't forget that you are almost fifteen years younger than I am. That still makes me feel guilty in the back of my mind for corrupting you, or at least for being a bad influence. Except for that fact, I'm thrilled and surprised that you want me as much as I want you. Being together with you just seems too good to be true."

"Now you are being silly about the age differential again. I already said that you are the perfect age for me. I'll tell you what we're going to do. After you finish your coffee, we will go lie down side by side in the bunk and take a nap since we will have a busy day ahead of us tomorrow. We can challenge ourselves to just hold each other and cuddle while we have a nice rest. We'll see how long we can last that way," she said with a wicked expression.

22

"I told you, resting this close together wasn't a good idea. I did have a wonderful dream about being with you all alone on an island, though. What time is it anyway?"

"It's one o'clock in the afternoon, Tom. We've been sleeping for four hours. Since we did so well cuddled up together without any hanky panky involved, we deserve to reward ourselves with a little more togetherness."

"I guess you were right about me needing more rest. I feel better after our nap, and I do want you more than can possibly be expressed in mere words. It might be time for me to begin some hands on physical therapy. Or maybe that should be hand on therapy until I can use both hands again. It will take a lot longer, but this time, I will take a turn at undressing both of us for a change. Then you can do that thing that you do so well. Once I undo all your buttons and remove your garments, then you can push my buttons all over again."

"It sounds like I'm finally having a positive influence on you. I never figured you for the amorous kind of guy. Now you're almost lapsing poetic on me and becoming a little bit daring to boot. I had you pegged as a cerebral type who kept everything bottled up inside. If you're not careful, I may end up knowing exactly how you feel about me."

"I'm sorry. I didn't mean to be mushy. I know I've never been accused of that before by anyone. Come over here and let me demonstrate how much I care for you so far. Then I'll be able to back off sufficiently to maintain an aura of mystique, which will keep you sufficiently interested."

"If you say so, but that would be totally unnecessary. You already have my undivided attention and all the enthusiasm I could possibly muster. I sure have mixed emotions about your one-handed approach, though. I want you to hurry up and get us both naked. At the same time, I want you to take all the time in the world to make it last forever so we can really savor our moments together. Mmmm, I have chills all over whenever you touch me that way. Don't you dare stop."

"You're going to have to quit moving like that. I almost had that little button undone. Why did they have to make all the button holes on your blouse so tiny? Maybe my fingers are too big for this sort of thing."

"If it was easy, anybody could do it. This way you can enjoy it more and have a better sense of accomplishment when you're done. If all else fails, it might be faster if you were to bite them off."

"If you don't stop holding my head against your chest, I may never finish getting you completely undone and fully accessible. Not that what you're doing doesn't feel absolutely wonderful, though."

"Sorry, I just can't wait to have you again. I hope I didn't hurt your shoulder."

"Nope, it must be healing because it isn't quite as painful all the time now, but if you don't stop pulling me to you, I might be sorely tempted to chew off your bra from the front."

Once Joan was back in position, she appeared to be slightly more aggressive than the day before, if that were somehow remotely possible. Because we had gotten to know each other in the most intimate detail, perhaps she felt more in control. She sure seemed to be certain of who she was now, along with knowing exactly what she wanted. I think we both were enjoying being together more this way now. We certainly were making it last infinitely longer so we could appreciate every minute we shared, each trying to please the other.

"Uncle already yet," I said as my good arm flopped down, too spent to continue.

"I'm sorry, did I hurt you? I thought you were having as much fun as I was," Joan said.

"I'm astonished that you haven't begun to approach the point of exhaustion that I reached some time back. This has been nothing short of phenomenal, but you know what they say about too much of a good thing?"

"No, what do *they* say about it?" she said, grinning as she proceeded to grind down against me anew.

"Well, for one thing, *they* say that sex is the one thing you can never get enough of until just after you've had it. Believe me when I tell you that we have really had it."

"You say that like it's a bad thing," she exclaimed as she continued moving on top of me without noticeably slowing down.

"It all has been extraordinary, and I mean that in the nicest, most delightful way possible. It does bring a new definition to the term *joined at the hip*. I'm almost reverting to the train of thought that it will never be possible for me to keep up with you."

"Don't you remember that since I saved your life, you are my responsibility? I'm doing my very level best to fulfill my obligation. You also seem to be forgetting you were shot a few days back, and it will be some time before you're back to your usual, loveable self."

"You don't need me to tell you that you are exceptionally good at what you do in any activity. If you remember correctly, we didn't start this before I was wounded, so you have no idea what my usual, loveable self looks like. As a matter of fact, after the last couple of days, I don't remember what I was like before, but I know that I've never felt this way before or with this much intensity."

"Hang on to that thought because as I've previously mentioned, I'm keeping score and you are going to owe me a bunch when you're back on your feet. Perhaps Peter Pickering had the right idea by writing everything down in a journal. When it's your turn to be in charge, I completely expect you to bring me to the same state of euphoria that you appear to be in now."

"Sounds like a tall order, but that can't happen until somewhere way down the road. We need to get a good night's sleep because tomorrow we have to get back to work on the case."

"In that instance, sweet prince, I must bid thee adieu 'til the morrow breaks. I shall go take a long hot shower to cleanse and purify my innermost thoughts, lest mine be corrupted were they to linger for too long a time inside my head. I will try not to wake thee when I get into my bunk tonight. Good night, darling. It's been wonderful."

"Good night, Joan. Until the morning comes then, my love."

23

"**G**ood morning, cutie. You look absolutely adorable, especially considering our get-acquainted marathon yesterday. You don't look even half as exhausted as I feel."

"Hi, honey. I'll take that as a compliment, I think. You didn't have to make breakfast. It couldn't have been easy using a whisk and only one arm."

"It was no big deal. They are only buttermilk pancakes from a box mix. You probably won't even notice the lumps. I told you I could take my turns with the cooking. Partners are supposed to share. There is a fresh pot of coffee on the stove when you're ready for it. I have Peter's journal and the Three P Company invoices to the Dutchman for cross references sorted out in my valise."

"You know, Tom, the coffee isn't half bad and the flapjacks are almost as good as the ones at IHOP. I do wish we had real maple syrup like they have in New England though. The Europeans have no idea what they're missing."

"Well, eat up. We don't know how bad the traffic will be between here and Zurich at this time of the day. I'd like to get an early start on the files with Rob and Alma."

"That was a pretty good breakfast, all things considered, Tom. Thank you very much," she said, giving me a kiss on the cheek.

"Did you have enough to eat? I have enough batter mixed to fry up a few more if you want."

"That was plenty. I'm stuffed. Let's just throw the dishes in the sink for now and be on our way."

We jumped into the Ford Focus with Joan behind the wheel as usual. I noticed that there was plenty of headroom for us to get in without ducking because of the arched roof. Then I realized that maybe I was more observant this morning because I wasn't in as much pain. Rolling my shoulder, it appeared that all of our activity in the bunk the last two days had loosened up the joints and muscles on the left side.

Slowly I clenched my fist, rotated my wrist, and flexed my elbow. Surprised at the range of motion today without the sheer agony experienced up until this point, I carefully slid my arm out of the sling.

Joan looked over, raised an eyebrow, and said, "Tom, what are you doing?"

I gingerly moved my arm and shoulder around. Cautiously, I lifted the sling over my head and said, "You really did take care of me after all. It had to be all those calisthenics you put us through at the hostel. I guess I do owe you big time after all, as you so eloquently put it."

"What do you mean? I think you should put that sling back on until your shoulder is completely healed."

As I experimented with moving my left side, I said, "My shoulder is still sore, but it doesn't hurt as much now. I think I'm ready to do without the sling. It will stiffen up if I don't start to use it more."

"Are you sure that won't set you back in the healing process," she said with her brow furled and a concerned look on her face.

"Yes, I am, but I also think you should keep your eye on the road," I said as she jerked the wheel to pull the car back to our side before we hit the Mercedes truck barreling down toward us on the narrow two-lane road.

"Boy, that was too close for comfort. I'm sorry, Tom. I was worried about your welfare and got sidetracked."

"That momentary distraction could have really put a damper on our accomplishments today. That's one of the reasons why I felt we could have problems working together if we developed an intimate relationship."

"I'm glad to know you feel we have progressed to a relationship phase, but I can easily get back on track and be more alert from now on. You just surprised me when you removed your sling. I thought you still needed to use it."

"If you're absolutely positive that you're okay with our age difference, I think we are beginning to feel the same way about each other. It just seems strange that it hit us both so hard and so fast. While I appreciate that you want to look after my well-being, we both will need to concentrate more on what we're doing when we're working on the case in the field."

"I'm sorry, Tom, I've never felt this way about anyone else before. It takes some getting used to. I think that's the building over there," she said, pulling into the one empty parking spot on the street.

"The sign in the second floor window says, 'Firma Interaktiv,' which would be abbreviated CIA in English. At least these agents haven't lost their sense of humor," I said as I pushed the bell to be buzzed in after they checked out the window to see who we were.

At the top of the stairs, we could see Rob at the computer keyboard and Alma pulling hard copies from the filing cabinets. "*Guten morgen*, I like your Company Inter Active sign on the window," I said as we entered the room.

"Good morning, that was Alma's idea," Rob said, looking up from the computer.

"Hello, it's good to see you again. There's a fresh pot of coffee over there on the sideboard cabinet if you'd like some," Alma said, trying to gesture with her hands full with a stack of papers.

"Here, let me help you," Joan said, rushing across the room to try to catch the pile as it started to slide.

"Thank you, I guess I shouldn't have tried to point while I was holding all those files," Alma said.

"No problem. Let me grab a cup of coffee, and I can give you a hand sorting them all out," Joan said with a pleasant smile. "Tom and I discussed what we might look for in van Rijn's Mikrowelle files.

"The one returned shipment tipped us off on the ultimate destination and return route, when the North Koreans made the mistake of ordering the wrong part number. We can document any invoices that Mikrowelle had trans-shipped via Hong Kong to have Alex's guys at Langley track the satellite images of ships and trains bound for North Korea on those dates.

"We only had the Three P Company's invoices and Pickering's journal to go by before, but now we can also check to see if Mikrowelle was ordering the same kind of goods from other suppliers."

"Sounds like a plan to me," Alma said.

"If Rob can print out the shipping records, I can look for shipments destined for Hong Kong in the hard copies while he searches for other pertinent files in van Rijn's office computer. First, I need another cup of coffee to see if I can get both eyes open at the same time," I said.

"I noticed you don't have your sling on today, Tom. Is the shoulder feeling better?" Rob asked.

"The pain seems to have subsided quite a bit. I must be finally on the mend, so I figured I'd see how I do without the extra support," I said. "Did you learn anything more from your questioning of Sang-hee?"

"Since she recently arrived in Switzerland, she didn't seem to know anything about the Dutchman or Peter Pickering. We have her life's history about how the North Koreans pulled her out of gymnastics training for the Olympics when she was in her early teens.

"They had her learn martial arts and other languages so she could become a government spy. She was duped into believing that placing the bomb that brought down the South Korean passenger flight would make her homeland a safer place.

"It wasn't until she had the opportunity to see what life was like in other countries that she realized how much she had been brainwashed with all their twisted propaganda.

"Apparently, they are amassing a treasure trove of information from her about how the government in North Korea really functions. Everything there is run from the top down and under tight control of their *Dear Leader*. We already knew most of that, but the new detailed input may be helpful to us down the road," Rob said.

The office was fairly quiet for the rest of the day while we combed and sifted through all the data. We assumed that we were not under surveillance. Just to be safe, we left the "office" when Rob and Alma locked up. They were on their way to the American embassy in Bern with all the information to be dispatched to the CIA headquarters in Langley.

On the way to the hostel, I realized that Peter's home office might have been ransacked by the North Koreans. It occurred to me that perhaps Maarten van Rijn had information that might be useful to us at his home in Ede, Holland.

"Joan, when we get back, why don't we try to book a flight to Amsterdam in the next day or two? Then we can go to van Rijn's house to see if we can find answers about what the North Koreans don't want us to know. We could be back in a day or two before Langley verifies where all those shipments of analog parts and components were going."

"That makes sense to me. The travel time would only be about an hour and a half each way, if we can make reservations on nonstop flights. I'll log on to book tickets as soon as we return to the hostel."

"I was thinking it might not be wise for us to take cabs to and from the train to Ede since we don't want to be tracked or seen. I'll check on car rental rates and room availability if we need to stay overnight. Ede is only an hour's drive from the airport in Amsterdam."

Back at our room, Joan turned away from her laptop and said, "The best I could do on short notice is KLM flight 1958 out of Zurich at noon tomorrow with a 12:15 PM return on KLM 1959 the following day. The flight to Amsterdam is on a 737-700, but the return says City Hopper. Do you want me to see what kind of plane that is?"

"Zurich to Amsterdam is a short flight, so it doesn't really matter. You can book those tickets with my credit card so it can all go on the same expense report. In the meantime, I'll find a rental car and hotel."

A short while later, she said, "We're good to go. After I change your dressings, we should get a good night's sleep so you'll be well rested for tomorrow. How did you make out?"

"I had trouble finding a room in Amsterdam. Apparently there's a citywide electronic music and dance festival going on called Five Days Off. I had to splurge on a five-star place called Hotel Pulitzer, but it's only for tomorrow night. The good news is that we only needed one room this time. How are we going to explain that on our expense report?"

"Hey, we've saved the government money so far by sharing a single room in the hostel. We can live it up for one night on their nickel. Besides, we're grown-ups. What happens between us behind closed doors is none of their business," she said with a twinkle in her eye as she wrapped her arms around me to share a prolonged kiss.

24

In the morning after breakfast, we decided we could make do with only one suitcase between us for an overnight stay in Amsterdam. I was uncomfortable with the fact that once again, we couldn't take our guns with us for our protection, but I didn't dare bring up the subject with Joan. We would just have to be more cautious.

The ride to the airport in Zurich seemed to take less time on this trip. With Joan concentrating on driving in the relatively light midmorning traffic, I had a chance to study her face in profile. It's amazing how much a little pain can dull all your other senses. Now that I was feeling better, I realized anew what a beautiful person she really was and not just on the outside. She was intelligent, articulate, and seemed to have a unique talent for becoming highly skilled fairly quickly at everything she attempted. Then I wondered what she could possibly see in me that she couldn't find in someone from her own age group. I had to ask myself, *If this thing between us did become more serious, how long could it possibly last?*

Lost in my thoughts, I was surprised when she said, "Tom, we're at the airport," when she couldn't get my attention.

"Oh, okay I'll get our bag from the trunk," I said, waking from my daydreaming and forcing myself to concentrate.

"Take your time. Just give me your passport, and I'll go on ahead to print out our boarding passes, then meet you at the KLM counter," she said as she took off at her usual brisk pace.

As I approached the ticket counter, she said, "How are you feeling without using the sling today?"

"I'm doing much better than yesterday. I've probably healed enough to have the stitches removed at this point."

Walking down the corridor to our gate, I felt naked after having a gun to carry for our protection since we went to the American Embassy in Bern the first time. If Joan had noticed my frequent, furtive glances to look for any sign of trouble, she didn't let on.

Each time she saw I was lagging behind, she patiently waited for me to catch up. "Are you okay? Do you want me to take the luggage?" she asked, looking concerned, putting a comforting hand on my arm.

"I'm fine. I just can't understand why you are always in such a rush to get somewhere, only to sit and wait when you get to your destination."

"I don't know why that is. I've always been in a hurry. I can try to change if it bugs you that much."

"Please don't ever change anything about you on my account. It's part of what makes you a unique individual. I like you just the way you are. I'm just trying to understand you better so I know what to expect."

"So now you want me to be predictable?" she asked, tossing her hair back and dazzling me with that radiant smile.

"No more than I am for you. I like the element of surprise and spontaneity about you. That's our gate over there on the right. It looks like they are already preparing to board."

Once she stowed our bag in the overhead compartment and were settled in our assigned seats, Joan asked, "Do you have enough room? How is your shoulder holding up?"

"You are going to have to stop worrying about me so much. The shoulder feels much better than it did just a few days ago. I have plenty of leg room.

"This reminds me of my last flight to New York City on Royal Dutch Airlines that I took to get home when I was still in the service. I was sitting next to a Dutchman when I noticed he had an eight-inch-by-three-inch pamphlet with page after page consisting of two columns. One side of each page had American words and terms and the other column was for the analogous English word or expression. I was astounded there were so many different idiosyncrasies between the United States and the United Kingdom.

"On that flight, KLM served a lettuce salad with a fish filet on top. I thought that was rather odd, but I tried it anyway. It was absolutely abominable. I immediately spit it back out into the plastic bag the silverware came in. I ate every last bit of the dinner they served and swallowed two cups of coffee. I still couldn't get rid of the terrible taste. Later I found out the Dutchman spoke enough English to tell me the filet was eel, which is considered a great delicacy in Europe. I should have asked him if he thought that was good eel. I still don't know if I like eel, because I never dared to try it again," I said.

I must have made a face when I shook my head at the memory because Joan broke out laughing at my recounting of the story and covered her mouth with her hand.

Even though this was a fairly short flight, KLM served hard rolls and cheese with the coffee. I mentioned that Hotel Pulitzer was located on a canal near Anne Frank's house and the Westerkerk Protestant church which was built in 1631. I also noted Rembrandt was buried there.

"How did you know about all that?" she asked.

"It was with the information I looked up on the Internet about the hotel," I responded with a knowing grin.

There was a little bit of a crosswind gusting during our runway approach at the Amsterdam airport, but it subsided enough to allow for a relatively smooth landing. They were right when they said that sometimes timing is everything.

I didn't have a problem pulling down our one bag from the overhead compartment with only my right arm. It was then

I noticed Joan must have dashed down the aisle to the front of the plane before the door was opened. A number of heads turned to give her dirty looks for not being polite enough to wait for her turn. She turned to see me watching her and gave me a little wave of her fingers. With a mischievous grin and a shrug of her shoulders, she dashed out the door ahead of everyone else.

Naturally she was first in line when I arrived at the car rental counter. In no time at all, we were underway. The drive to the center of the city to reach the Hotel Pulitzer was quick. Checking in, I asked where we could find a restaurant in the area with a touch of old world charm. They recommended a place called the Five Flies. Supposedly when it opened in the seventeenth century, the original owner was always busy, buzzing around, so he was nicknamed the Fly.

Calling the restaurant for a reservation, I discovered they didn't open until 6:00 PM, so we had more than enough time on our hands before dinner. We put that to good use, now that I was more agile than before. Although our pace was slightly subdued compared to our initial introduction to sharing passion, it wasn't any less intense. That was followed by a leisurely shower together and a nap, nestled in each other's arms.

Waking refreshed, we walked to the restaurant on Spiustraat, only to be surprised that the sign on the door at the end of the alley said, "Born 1627." According to the literature I read while waiting for our table to be cleared, there were four original Rembrandt etchings in the room bearing his name. After being greeted by a suit of armor, the numerous antiques and large splashes of red color accentuating the highly polished dark wood walls with attractive lighting all combined to create a festive atmosphere.

Because of the large variety of choices on the menu, we decided to take a chance with the "four-course surprise." The food was anything but disappointing. Unfortunately, we left the table a little too full to be comfortable. If we ever return, we'll have to pace ourselves better.

Returning to the hotel, we were fully sated with food and each other. Stripping out of our clothes, we slid under the sheets and rolled over into a gentle embrace. After another full day of activity, we drifted off to a blissful sleep, happy to have been able to enjoy the experiences together.

25

Breakfast was included with the price of the deluxe room package at the Pulitzer Hotel. The dining room walls consisted of dark walnut inlaid panels with carved ornate moldings illuminated by sparkling, multifaceted crystal chandeliers. The silver salt and pepper shakers, sugar bowls, creamers, and utensils shined as if they were freshly polished. Everything was immaculate, the staff attentive, the linens fresh and the food superb. Nothing was overlooked that would detract from the dining experience, even for breakfast.

Walking out later, we were surprised that not only did the concierge ask if we needed directions, but he also knew our names and spoke impeccable English. We had observed him in action the evening before. It seemed he greeted everyone by name in their native tongue and must have been fluent in eight or ten languages. He inquired of each returning guest how they had enjoyed their museum visit or wherever they had been. His memory and attention to detail were nothing short of amazing.

The trip to Ede didn't take long. It was situated where forest began at the edge of the Dutch plains. On the way into town coming off the A12 motorway, we saw the Kimberly-Clark headquarters buildings. Locating the van Rijn house wasn't difficult, but the front door was locked.

Going around to the back, we found the rear door ajar with the glass window smashed. Because we didn't have our weapons with us, we were extremely cautious as we entered together and explored each room.

Everything was trashed, but at least we were convinced that the house was empty, except for us. Books and papers were strewn about everywhere. All the fabric covers for the mattresses, sofas, and chairs were slashed open in the search for something. Drawer contents were unceremoniously dumped in heaps on the floor.

"Well, it looks like we're a day late and a Euro short again," I said, looking around. "Let's see if we can find anything useful to us they might have missed. Unless their objective was to destroy everything, it looks like they didn't find what they were after. Maybe we can succeed where they failed."

We wandered from room to room, turning over everything for careful examination while being careful not to leave any fingerprints behind. Walking past the small fireplace in the den, I heard the floorboards creak underfoot. Joan helped me turn the love seat upright and move it off the large oriental area rug. Then we rolled the carpet out of the way.

Sure enough, there were scratches on the edges of the old lacquered boards. We pried the loose boards up with the point of a poker from the hearth only to discover a small leather briefcase in a cavity between the floor joists.

We had no way of knowing how long ago the house had been ransacked or who tore it apart. Since we had already explored all the rooms, we decided to put the few things that we had moved back to the way we had found them. We quickly left with the briefcase before anyone showed up so we didn't have to answer any questions and be detained.

Having spent so much time going through the mess at van Rijn's house, we would be cutting it close to be able to catch our scheduled flight back to Zurich. We decided it would be safer to wait until we returned to Switzerland before sorting out whatever was inside the black leather case.

The intermittent rain we encountered on the way back to the airport wasn't enough to slow us down. The gray skies cast a dismal hue over all the flowers we saw starting to bloom in the yards and fields. There was no indication along the way that anyone was following us.

After dropping Joan off with the luggage, I checked the car back in at the rental lot. I didn't complain this time about how fast Joan was moving down the terminal to get to the gate. We were fortunate that people with American passports were given preferential treatment in clearing security.

Essentially they announced that anyone with an American passport come to a separate line. Once there we merely held them up as they waved us through. Maybe they were too far behind in boarding all the flights.

Because we only had the one piece of luggage and the briefcase, there was no question about the number of carry-on bags we had between us. The boarding of our flight had already begun when we arrived, so we were able to go directly to our seats.

As soon as we were buckled in our seat belts, Joan took my hand, looked up at me with those beautiful brown eyes, and asked, "How are you doing?"

"I already told you when you asked earlier this morning. I'm feeling much better. My shoulder almost seems to be back to normal, but thanks for asking."

At that, she smiled and sat back in her seat but didn't relinquish her grip on my hand. Holding hands felt like the natural thing for us to do. Her hand felt warm and tender as I gave it a little squeeze. It was amazing that we could have developed deep feelings for each other so quickly. I had resigned myself to being a loner, but maybe this thing that had developed between us was meant to be on some cosmic plain.

There still was a light drizzle falling under dark, overcast skies when we touched down on the tarmac in Switzerland. Joan didn't bolt down the aisle this time when the seat belt light went off. She seemed reluctant to let go of my hand. I wasn't in a hurry to break the mind-set connection we had established between us either.

Once through the gate, we again held hands as we slowly walked toward long-term parking to pick up the Focus. It seemed we were becoming attached to the rental car as much as each to other.

I think we both felt more secure once we retrieved our weapons from the trunk. I suspect we were both anxious to return to the hostel to see what was in the briefcase. Joan said she didn't want to stop to eat on the return from Zurich. Late afternoon traffic was relatively light on the way back, and we made good time.

Once we were in our room, we made sandwiches with lettuce, tomato, and cold cuts to go with our freshly brewed coffee. Then we proceeded to pry open the locks on the briefcase with a Swiss Army knife we found in a drawer of a kitchen cabinet. Spreading the contents of the case over the table, we sorted the invoices we found inside alphabetically by company name.

Oddly enough, one manila folder contained an agreement with Peter's Three P Company whereby van Rijn would receive a 15 percent discount on all orders as long as he continued to deal exclusively with Peter. Obviously, the Dutchman wasn't holding up his end of the bargain but was pocketing the discount anyway.

Based on what we found, most of the van Rijn orders were direct shipped from the States to the Lotus Trading Company in Taipei, Taiwan, instead of consolidating orders in Europe first from multiple suppliers. That way, the need to pay the duties in Europe was avoided. Of course it also cut into Peter's profit margin on the diminished Three P dealings.

"I'll bet the CIA will be glad to hear about van Rijn's double dipping with other vendors at Peter's expense when they get the list of the rest of the suppliers," I said to Joan.

"Not only that, we don't know how many others are involved in sending parts and components to North Korea besides van Rijn, if any," she said.

"We have stacks of invoices on the table from eleven different distributors scattered around the United States. Apparently North Korea didn't want the US to know what they were doing by converting our commercial and domestic products into weapons systems to use against us and threaten the South Koreans. They probably figured it would be easier to replace their sources than to come up with technical alternatives if their ruse was discovered."

"We should alert Alex to watch for other shipping company agents of analog parts and components who suddenly disappear. Maybe they can also track down orders with digital

elements that are being shipped to North Korea for finished assemblies of autos, business machines, appliances, and industrial equipment.

"I'm kind of tuckered out. Why don't we make a list of topics to discuss on our next conference call with Alex, Alma and Rob first thing in the morning?" I said.

"I think I'm about ready to turn in after a long day too. How is your shoulder feeling by the way?"

"It still feels much better. Why do you keep asking about it?"

"I was just thinking that if you could help me with taking down the frame of the top bunk, we could put the two beds on the floor side by side. It might be tight to walk past it during the daytime, but it would be a lot easier for us to cuddle without falling off the edge of the bed."

"Okay, let's go for it. As tired as I feel, I don't think I'll have much of a problem getting to sleep tonight though."

26

"Good morning, Tom. I was wondering when you were going to get those adorable baby blues of yours wide open. I knew you were in there somewhere behind that silly grin you had on your face."

"Hi there, beautiful, how come you are wide awake, bright-eyed, bushy-tailed, and in such a good mood this morning already?"

"I've been fully conscious for some time now. First I was thinking how nice it was to wake up right next to you without being in danger of falling over the edge of a single crowded bunk. Second, I figured it was my turn to gaze at you for a change while I contemplated how I want to ravage you later," she said with her megawatt smile.

"Does that mean you actually liked what you saw?"

"I decided that with you I finally got lucky. I'm so glad we met and had a chance to get to know each other like this. Thank you for being who you are."

"When you put it that way, I'm happy that we met too. It sure is different being with a lover who can relate to where I'm coming from and what I do on the job. I've never met anyone like you before, and that's an absolutely wonderful thing."

"Have you considered the possibility that you might just be delusional?" she said as she hauled off and walloped me in the face with the feather pillow.

"So far it does seem to be a dream with some sort of special magical aspects involved. Perhaps you are a figment of my imagination that I conjured up because someone as nice as you are couldn't exist in the real world," I said.

"Do you have a shovel under your side of the bed, or did you fall off your bunk and land on your head during the night? Where is all that stuff coming from?"

"Hey, maybe it's way too soon for us to have a conversation like this. I guess what I'm trying to say is that I feel we're off to a great start and look forward to see where we go from here. Let's discuss what direction our investigation should precede over a leisurely breakfast.

"One name that would crop up frequently when I was reviewing Peter's logbook was Elektronikindustrie up in Basel. We could visit them to find out when Peter was last there and what they specialize in. Another major customer appeared to be an outfit called Steuerung down in Lucerne.

"We could drive up to Basel while Rob and Alma check out Lucerne. Then we can meet them in Lucerne to compare notes while we finish mapping out a plan of action. By the time we get back, the results we are waiting to hear about from Langley may be available," I said.

"That sounds good to me, Tom. Why don't you give them a call while I get everything ready for the Basel trip? If you are up to it, maybe we can share the driving this time."

"That would be welcome change. I was getting tired of just riding shotgun when you have the GPS to navigate. We don't even need road maps for these trips anymore. If you don't mind, I'll take the first leg to Basel."

"Did you enter the location for Elektronikindustrie in the GPS?" I asked.

"Yep, we're all set to go. With me driving, it would only take a little over an hour to get there. With you behind the wheel, we might arrive in time for lunch, if we're lucky."

"Now that was uncalled for. When I drove the other day, I was still wearing a sling and maneuvering through heavy city traffic only using one arm."

"I'm sorry, I couldn't resist. You're such an easy target because you are so serious all the time," Joan said as she kissed her fingertips and touched them to my lips.

"Okay, I'll try to lighten up from now on. In the meantime, why don't you do something useful instead? You can watch to make sure nobody is following us along the way."

"*Jawohl, mein Kapitan!* It shall be done as you command," she said, saluting while trying to not break into a grin.

"And here I thought we were getting along so well with everything going smoothly."

We found Elektronikindustrie tucked in the back of an industrial park. At the receptionist's desk, we asked to see Herr Schneider since his name was the only one in Peter's journal and on all the shipping documents for this firm. When the statuesque woman with the braided flaxen hair in a bun returned, she said in admirable English, "He will see you now. Please follow me."

Upon introductions, Herr Schneider insisted we call him Gunter. I informed him that Peter Pickering had an accident and couldn't remember what had happened. We explained that we were trying to retrace his steps to see if that information might jog his memory.

Gunter said when Peter didn't show up there for his last appointment, he became worried. He said it wasn't like him at all. Peter would always call if he was going to be the least little bit late or reschedule immediately if something unforeseen came up.

Following an elongated discussion of exactly what comprised the core of Elektronikindustrie's business, we thanked Gunter profusely for his time and assured him we would ask Peter to get back in touch with him when he was doing better.

On the way out to the rental car, it started to sprinkle. Before we could make our way across the parking lot, it was coming down in buckets. On the run, I hollered above the rolling thunder to make myself heard. Since we had agreed that Joan would take a turn driving, I handed her the keys with both of us in full stride. Because there wasn't much taper in her skirt, I was amazed that fact didn't seem to slow her down at all, especially wearing high heels.

Ducking into the car, she looked so adorable with her hair soaking wet and water dripping off her face that I leaned over to give her a kiss. "What was that for?" she said. "I thought we agreed that we were going to keep business separate from pleasure."

"So you're trying to say you don't think I mean business where you are involved?"

"It so happens that I agreed with you that we needed to establish boundaries if we are ever going to be able to make this arrangement between us work."

"Okay, I'll admit that it was a pleasure, but you looked so cute dripping wet with your hair curling up like that, I just couldn't resist. I'll make an extra effort to be more professional from now on. Then you won't file a sexual harassment suit against me," I said, grinning.

"Tom, the only suit of mine that I want against you is my birthday suit," Joan said with a chuckle while licking her lips.

With that thought, I leaned back against the headrest, closed my eyes, and contemplated where that vision could ultimately lead.

27

As we approached the Belchen tunnel on the A2 Motorway headed for Chiasso we saw an old woman dressed completely in white, trying to hitchhike a ride. Joan mumbled that we couldn't leave her stranded out in the pouring rain, so she pulled over to the side of the road. Joan backed up, and the woman got in the rear seat. Joan waited for a break in traffic and got up to speed again on the way toward the tunnel.

The old lady did not look well, so I inquired if she was feeling okay.

In a quivering voice, she said to me, "Someone close to you is going to disappear."

I turned to ask what she meant by that, and she had somehow vanished mysteriously. Because I felt so sleepy, I thought I must have dreamed all that so I didn't mention anything to Joan about it. I just put my head back to resume my nap.

As hard as it was raining when we entered the tunnel, it seemed strange as we emerged into bright sunshine two miles later. I told Joan that perhaps the local weather system behaves like the snow in the Berkshire Mountain Range. Pittsfield, Massachusetts, is surrounded by mountains. Every cloud in the winter dumps snow into the mountainous bowl that envelopes the city. Meanwhile, thirty miles to the north, Bennington, Vermont, is open on the west side. Almost all the snow up there is dumped on the other side of the mountains from Bennington, which makes for happy skiers in those areas. The Bennington residents are pleased that they don't need to shovel snow as much as their neighbors in Pittsfield to the south.

We kept going until we reached the place we had agreed upon to meet in Lucerne. Alma and Rob were already seated, having coffee.

As we joined them at the table, the waitress brought menus and asked if we wanted coffee. Once that was out of the way, Rob asked if we ran into the bad storms predicted up in the Basel area. When I casually mentioned I had a dream about an old woman I saw hitchhiking in the heavy rain near the Belchen tunnel entrance, Rob asked, "Was she dressed all in white, and did she vanish after she gave you a warning?"

"Yes, she was wearing all white clothing, and yes, she did disappear from the back seat after we stopped to offer her a ride. How could you possibly know that?" I inquired.

"You've got to be kidding me. Are you serious or is this a joke?" Rob asked with a puzzled look.

"I don't think Tom has heard about her, Rob," Alma said, grabbing his arm.

"Heard what about her? Is she a serial killer or something?" I said now that Rob had piqued my curiosity.

"You just described seeing the white lady, who is locally known as the Weisse Frau. She's a ghost that haunts the tunnel to warn people when something really dreadful is going to happen. At least that's how the story goes," Rob said.

"Is that coffee you are drinking in your cup, or did you add something extra to it?" I asked incredulously.

"Hey, I'm not making this up. Ask Alma. This is local folk lore," Rob said in a sincere tone of voice.

Joan sat patiently through all of this discussion and then said, "I think Tom was having a dream episode while I was driving."

"Well, as much fun as this conversation has been, why don't we order so we can talk about what we learned today," I said.

Over dinner, Alma said they visited the company called Steuerung in Lucerne and found out Peter had visited there on schedule the day before he disappeared. There was nothing odd or unusual. The company primarily deals with controls for steering and navigation. They didn't know where their shipments go once they reach the trading companies in the Far East, but most were delivered to a company called Lotus in Taiwan.

"At least you got some information about Peter Pickering's route on his last visit to Switzerland. We went to Elektronikindustrie in Basel only to find he didn't show up for his appointment a few days after his disappearance. They handle multilayer circuit boards and control panel assemblies," Joan said.

Handing Rob the list, I said, "Here are the American companies that we found out the Dutchman was dealing with. As I mentioned to you on the phone, the briefcase was the only thing we found that might be useful to us in his house. Maybe you could arrange to dust his house for prints in Ede, Holland. Then we might find out who trashed the place."

"So as far as we know, all the analog products the Three P Company distributes could go into replacing the digital components for use in weapon systems for North Korea. We'll have to keep digging. Have you heard how Peter is doing, by the way?" I asked.

Rob volunteered that he seems to recognize his wife Monique most of the time now, but his memory is still hazy on most everything else so far.

"Has Langley been able to track the Three P Company shipments to North Korea with the satellite photographs yet?" I asked.

"Not completely, but they're still working on it."

"Well, it was great seeing you two again. As usual, you've been a big help. Thank you," I said, shaking hands.

Joan followed suit, and we went back to the car. "It's been a long day. Are you still up to driving?"

"Sure, no problem at all, I've been feeling better each day," I said.

Joan reset the GPS for the hostel, and we were underway. Back on the road, Joan reached over to hold my hand after we were up to speed on the highway and the car was in fifth gear.

Once we had returned to the hospice, Joan said, "Your shoulder looked much improved the last time I changed your bandages. Let me see if the wounds have healed sufficiently to consider removing your stitches."

"The front closed up nicely. How is the back doing?

"I think it's ready. Let me snip the stitches with the scissors and pull them out. Then you'll be all set," she said.

"There you go, you're almost as good as new. I'll just put smaller bandages on both sides of your shoulder."

"Thank you, that feels a lot better. Now it doesn't pull when I move my arm."

Having driven a full loop on the roads in Switzerland, we were both exhausted so we decided to go to bed early.

28

It took a minute for me to realize that my cell phone was ringing. Joan's head was lying on my right arm with my back against the wall. Still half asleep, I extracted my arm and tried to crawl over her to get to the telephone without disturbing her. Instead, she wrapped both arms around my neck, arched her back, and pulled me down to her.

"Joan, my phone is ringing."

"Oh, and I was having the most delicious dream about you," she said sleepily with a crooked smile that made her look like the cat that just swallowed a canary.

It was still ringing by the time I reached the table. Fumbling with the buttons in the dark, I somehow managed to push the right one and said, "Hello."

"Tom, how are you doing? This is Alex."

"Alex? Are you still at the office this late? It's 4:00 AM here."

"Yeah, we were reviewing the satellite photographs of Taiwan that coincided with the delivery times of the shipments from the Three P Company. Without exception, there were ships, trains, and planes bound for North Korea shortly after. We're convinced it is not coincidental, so your investigation should focus on the North Koreans being behind all of this."

"Okay, Alex, thank you for the feedback. That's good to know."

"How is your shoulder doing, by the way?"

"Great. I've been getting around without the sling and just had the stitches taken out. It feels much better now."

"What did you learn from your trip to Basel about Pickering's travels before he was attacked?"

"He was a no-show for his appointment there. His customer said that was extremely uncharacteristic of Peter. Alma and Rob confirmed he was in Lucerne the day before he disappeared. They will be sending you the list of the eleven suppliers in the United States the Dutchman was dealing with separate from Peter that we know about. Since van Rijn's house in Ede, Holland was ransacked, we also asked Rob to have the place dusted for fingerprints."

"That's all good information. I'm sure it will help determine exactly who is behind all of this. Thanks, Tom, keep up the good work. You and Joan seem to work very well as a team together."

"We'll keep you posted on anything else we learn. Now go get some sleep, Alex."

Joan sat up on the bunk, yawned, stretched her arms, and said, "What's new with Alex?"

"All the satellite information on shipments from Taipei only points to North Korea's programs to build up their arsenal and to sell weapons to terrorists and third-world countries. Since I'm wide awake now, I might as well review my notes to see if there's something we missed in all of this. By the way, Alex thinks we fit together very well."

"He's sure got that right. If he only knew," she said. Being her usual exuberant self, Joan bounced up to greet me with a grin followed by a big hug and a good morning kiss. "While you're doing that, I'll fix us some breakfast. By the way, the larder is getting bare. I'll run out to get more supplies after we eat."

"Joan, I don't know what you do differently than I do, but your French toast is much better than what I usually make. What's your secret?"

"I just turn down the heat a little to cook them slower and add a little bit of love," she said as she rose to give me a kiss and stack the dishes in the sink.

"I'll try to remember that when it's my turn to cook again."

29

I was so absorbed in trying to make sense of all the data we had amassed; some time had elapsed before I realized that Joan had not returned from the marketplace. I was reluctant to call the local police and hospitals since we were trying to keep a low profile. Not knowing what else to do, I called Rob to see if he or Alma had been in touch with her.

They hadn't heard from Joan, but Rob said he had a contact at Hertz. Apparently, they can turn on a satellite-based GPS tracking system to pinpoint the location of their rental cars when they are overdue or stolen. He said he'd check and get back to me.

Waiting for minutes that seemed like hours, I began to realize how much Joan had really come to mean to me. I couldn't bear the thought of possibly losing her, so I started to berate myself for letting her go out alone. In the midst of my anguish, my cell phone rang. It was Rob. The coordinates for our rental car put it across the border on the outskirts of Schaffhausen inside the edge of a forest. He said he and Alma would come by to pick me up as soon as they could make it here.

Time seemed to drag as all kinds of terrible thoughts on Joan's fate flew viciously through my mind. I nervously checked to see if the clip in my gun was full, even though I knew it was. I became aware of an annoying drumming sound, only to realize it was my fingers on the table. Losing track of time, I paced in a circle long enough to wear a hole in the rug while I waited for them to show up. I began to wonder about the warning from the woman in white. Surely I must have dreamed that when I fell asleep in the tunnel. What didn't make sense was how did I know about the legend? I don't remember ever reading about it. Perhaps I had in the distant past and merely forgotten.

I had worked myself into such an anxious state that the knock on the door startled me. When I threw the door open, Rob was standing there. He said, "Come on, let's go."

We crossed the Rhine on Zollstrasse in the southwest section of Neuhausen and proceeded up to the plateau toward the Hoher Tanden summit. With Alma guiding us using her GPS screen, I was getting impatient until I spotted our rental car down a long dirt driveway in the woods.

"There's the Focus!" I shouted, trying to remain calm while pointing in the direction of the log cabin at the end of the narrow lane. I was glad that the car windows were rolled up so everyone in the vicinity didn't hear me.

Rob pulled off the main road and parked out of sight in the bushes between the trees just past the entrance road. He said, "We don't know how many people are in there or what we're up against. I don't see any other cars around. Give me five minutes to circle around back, and we'll all go in at the same time."

Alma and I slowly took turns running from tree to tree, pausing to duck behind the bushes along the way. One last check of my watch told me that Rob should be at the back door by now, so Alma covered me while I made a mad dash to the front door. It was unlocked, so I signaled for Alma to join me as I lifted the latch and nudged the door open with my shoulder as quietly as I could.

Tiptoeing through the cabin, we met Rob coming in from the back. Stopping to listen carefully, there was no sound coming from the open loft above, which ran around the perimeter of the room. Cautiously, I slowly opened the door to the cellar and froze as it made a creaking noise.

Peaking down into the dimly lit root cellar, I could see Joan slumped over in a chair with her hands tied behind her. She had a blindfold over her eyes, and her face appeared to be cut and swollen.

When my eyes adjusted to the darkness better, I could make out her captor, apparently asleep, leaning back in a chair, arms folded with a hat pulled down over his eyes. Filled with rage, I flew down the stairs and started to pummel this guy who had beaten her face to a pulp until Rob and Alma pulled me off him.

Rob said, "Tom, Tom. We're not going to learn anything from this creep if he's dead."

It was then that I heard a soft moan emanating from Joan. I rushed to her side and carefully removed her blindfold. After I untied her, she was only half-conscious as I helped her up the stairs. Using the hand pump mounted on the sink, I ran water over a towel, squeezed out the excess, and carefully dabbed it on her wounds.

Joan was coming to as I cradled her in my arms. "Joan, are you all right?" I whispered quietly, praying she had no serious injuries.

Her right eye was badly bruised and almost shut, but she was able to squint out of her left. Turning her head to get a look at me she said, "Tom, is that you? Thank heaven. I knew you'd come for me."

"I had to. I'm supposed to be looking after you," I said, trying to suppress my anger over what they had done to her.

Managing a half smile, she said, "I need a little water, my mouth is so dry."

Leaning her back in the chair, I grabbed a glass from the shelf and filled it from the pump. Gently lifting it to her split lips, she coughed and sputtered before managing to swallow a few gulps.

It was then that Alma came running back into the house out of breath. "We've got the guy tied up in the car. How's Joan doing?"

"I don't know yet. I'm still trying to find out," I said.

"I'll be okay," Joan stammered as she tried to stand before falling back into the chair.

"I don't think so. If I can find the keys to the car, I'm driving you straight to the Zurich University Hospital," I said.

"Oh, I've got them right here. They were in the guy's pocket," Alma said. If you think you can manage with her by yourself, I'll go with Rob and our prisoner to find out what this was all about. Let me give you a hand getting her out to the car first."

"Thanks, Alma. It looks like she took quite a beating," I said.

We helped her up and supported Joan on each side while walking her out to the car.

"I'll be fine," Joan said. "I just need a little rest."

"I doubt that partner. Just lean back and try to relax while I get you to the hospital. I don't want any arguments from you about it," I said.

"Okay, you're in charge," she said, closing her eyes.

30

I resisted the urge to run all the red traffic lights while I kept looking over to Joan to make sure she was okay. Both her eyes were shut, but I kept hearing soft moans and whimpers that she seemed to be unsuccessfully trying to suppress.

Arriving at the emergency room with the hazard flashers blinking, I honked the horn several times and ran inside to have them bring out a gurney. They wheeled her into the triage area when I was approached by a member of the Zurich Police Force. Of course he wanted to know what had happened to Joan and why my knuckles were skinned up.

I said she had been mugged in Platzspitz Park, and I fought off her attacker, but he escaped. He didn't seem to fully believe I shouldn't be the prime suspect in her beating. I told him I wanted to be alone with her right now so I asked him if he would please have Captain Johann Munzinger contact me later. I explained that we had met upon our arrival in Zurich, and he should tell him I am Tom Powers from the United States.

Hurrying back to the triage area of the emergency care treatment section, they were checking her vital signs and wheeling a portable X-ray machine over to her hospital bed. I was joined by a young pretty receptionist with a clipboard who was anxious to record all the pertinent details about Joan's history. I explained that Joan's pocketbook was stolen in the robbery, but I would obtain her insurance information for them.

I was shooed out of the emergency room to a waiting area where I called Alma. After explaining where we were, I asked how I could get the policy numbers and contacts the hospital required. She said she'd get back to me as soon as she could.

I was so antsy worrying about Joan that I couldn't sit still. The staff was probably wondering who the loony toon was that kept pacing in a circle like an expectant father.

About an hour later, Alma called back with the medical coverage data for all the hospital expenses. She then asked how Joan was doing. I told her I didn't have any feedback on her condition or prognosis yet.

As I was hanging up after the call, Captain Munzinger walked through the door. I explained to him everything that had happened. I also gave him the coordinates of the cottage where Joan was taken after she was kidnapped so he could check for clues. I suggested that it would probably work out better if we kept the whole thing quiet until we determined if there were more people involved. I thanked him for his discretion and said we'd keep him informed on any progress we have on the case.

After a couple more hours had passed, a serious-looking bespectacled doctor in blue scrubs with his mask and stethoscope still draped from his neck approached me from the emergency room. He informed me that the X-rays and MRIs did not show any signs of breaks, fractures, or concussions. He asked if she had lost consciousness, but I said I didn't know.

Although Joan had been badly beaten, which resulted in many bruises and cuts, he said she should heal completely in a few weeks. Except for one severe gash over her left eyebrow that required sutures, the rest of the wounds were pulled together with butterfly stitches.

"How long will she be staying in the hospital?" I asked anxiously.

"I would like to at least keep her overnight for observation. We will see how she is doing in the morning," he said with just a trace of a French accent.

"Is there any chance I can talk to her tonight?" I half-pleaded.

"I am sorry. She is under fairly heavy sedation to relieve the pain after her traumatic experience. It would be better if she was allowed to sleep undisturbed for the time being."

"Thank you so much for taking care of her, doctor," I said, shaking his hand.

I checked at the nurses' station before leaving to find out what time I could visit Joan in the morning. The second nurse I asked was fluent in English.

Once I got back to the hostel, I didn't know what to do with myself. Except for the night I'd spent in the Berkshire Medical Center, this was the first time Joan and I had been apart since the day we met. All of a sudden, it hit me like a ton of bricks how close the two of us had become in such an extremely short period of time. If Rob and Alma hadn't stopped me from beating up the slimeball who had interrogated her when they did, I probably would have killed him with my bare hands.

I realized that I should be trying to figure out who was behind all this and how to stop it. Unfortunately I couldn't concentrate on anything other than how much I wanted her to come out of this okay and how badly I missed her when she disappeared. All I could think about was Joan lying helpless and hurt in a hospital bed. I would have given anything if it was me in there instead of her having to bear all the pain.

My thoughts drifted back to the conversations we'd had about not getting involved with a partner. What good would I be in a firefight if I was distracted to the point where my main focus was how to protect Joan from harm? I now knew that I could no longer be rational and detached as far as Joan's safety was concerned. Wouldn't she be faced with the same dilemmas if the situation was reversed?

As much as I had developed deep feelings for this wonderful woman, I had to ask myself if I was crazy feeling the way I do. I still couldn't help thinking that she deserved someone who could provide a lot more on a long-term basis than what I had to offer. Not finding any answers that made sense, at some point during the night, I must have finally drifted off to a fitful sleep.

31

"**G**ood morning, Joan, are you feeling any better today?" I asked.

"Hi, Tom, it's too soon to tell yet. I feel like I've been run over by a cement truck. Boy, I'm so sore all over. I'd love to have you give me a kiss, but I don't think I can point to a spot that doesn't hurt."

"Well, since you brought me Dunkin' Donuts coffee when I was in the hospital, I checked to see if I could find one here. It appears they're all over Europe except in Switzerland. The nearest place was a two-hour round trip to Stuttgart in Germany so you'll have to settle for coffee and Cronuts from Migros."

"If that was supposed to be funny, please try to not make me laugh. Everything hurts too much. Migros sounds like a Greek yogurt, and I'll bite…what the heck is a Cronut?"

"Migros is a huge Swiss supermarket chain. The name comes from a combination of French words that mean halfway to wholesale. Likewise, Cronut is a hybrid pastry halfway between and croissant and a doughnut invented by a Frenchman in New York City. Unfortunately for him, his competition is copying his product and trademark without taking a license. Migros is supposed to be coming up with their own brand name for them. Aren't you sorry you asked?"

"Okay, it sounds intriguing, but I don't know if I can open my mouth wide enough without my lips cracking any more than they are already."

"No problem. I'll cut it up for you," I said, wishing I could relieve some of her pain.

No sooner did I start to spoon-feed her small bits of Cronuts that she washed down with sips of lukewarm coffee through a bent straw, when Alma showed up with a cardboard tray of coffees and a box of doughnuts from a local bakery.

"You'd better be really, really hungry with all this. By the way, I sure hope you don't feel as bad as you look," she said, laughing and giving Joan a hug while trying to minimize contact at the same time.

"What do you mean? How...how bad do I look?" Joan stammered. "Find me a mirror so I can see for myself."

"If you insist, I'll go try to find one, but you're the last person on Earth I would have expected to be concerned about her appearance. You always seem to be so confident and self-assured," Alma said.

While Alma headed off down the hallway to the nurses' station, I continued to feed Joan. It was then I noticed that her right eye had completely closed today and the swelling on her face hadn't started to subside yet.

Alma came back into the room with what looked like a little girl's toy hand mirror framed in pink plastic. Joan quickly snatched it from Alma's hand and tried to see her face through her good eye that was partially open. Holding it out at arm's length, she started to frown until she noticed Alma was taking out her cell phone. "Just what do you think are you doing?" Joan demanded to know, surprising Alma.

"I was just going to take a *before* picture so you can look back in a week or two and see how much you've improved," Alma replied innocently.

"Don't you dare do any such thing! Not if you value your life, Alma MacIntosh. If my dad ever saw how badly I was beaten, I'd never hear the end of it. As it is now, he worries about me far too much already," Joan said, apparently with real concern.

"Okay, okay, I'm sorry. We'll skip the *before* part then and concentrate on getting you sufficiently recuperated to take a decent looking *after* photo instead," Alma said meekly, not wanting to upset Joan any more than necessary.

"That's all right. I'm still kind of in a state of shock after everything that happened. By the way, where's Rob?" Joan asked.

"He's with Interpol and the Zurich police looking for clues and taking fingerprints at the cottage to see if we can't find the SOBs responsible for doing this to you. Do you know if there was more than one person involved?" Alma asked.

"The short, chunky guy with the moon face tried to interrogate me. He looked like he could have been Chinese. He spoke English with a strong accent, but he talked like his mouth was full of marbles.

"The other one was taller and lanky with a lot of tattoos of Asian symbols on his arms and neck. He had a high forehead, thin wispy hair in a ponytail and wore wire-rimmed glasses. He also looked Asian, but I wasn't sure if he was Chinese as well. I didn't think he looked Korean. He drove my car out to the cabin but left in a black sedan after we arrived. Both looked to be fairly young, maybe in their late twenties or early thirties," Joan said with great difficulty because her mouth was so sore from the severe beatings she endured.

"We've got the short, stocky one in custody that your partner here tried to kill when he saw what the sleaze ball had done to you. We can put an all-points bulletin out for the other one if he shows up on the surveillance film from the market place where they grabbed you. Maybe we can find his prints and get a picture of him too," Alma said.

"Meanwhile, we don't know why you were kidnapped or how they found out what we were doing. It's probably a good thing we got you out of the cottage before the other guy came back. We need to get you checked out of here before they find you again," I said.

"I didn't tell them anything, but they knew we are working for the United States Government," Joan said. "They kept asking me the same questions over and over and hit me every time I refused to answer."

"What else did they ask you?" I said.

"They wanted to know who I worked for, the name of my superiors, my objectives, and what department was I in."

"I hate to put you through all of this in your condition, but was their anything else you can remember?" I asked.

"Oh, they did keep asking me about Pickering, van Rijn, Park Min-ho, and Kang Sang-hee. Each time I responded with 'Who?' or 'I've never heard of them,' I would be hit again."

"I'm sorry you had to relive all that again, but at least that tells us something about what they know and what they were after. Since they realize what you and the rental car look like, we'd better get you to someplace safe before they start checking hospitals," I said.

"I can help there. I have an apartment down in Lucerne where you could stay until you get back on your feet again," Alma said.

"That's okay, we can find another place. We appreciate the offer, but we don't want to become a burden for you," Joan said.

"It's no problem. I have a spare bedroom, and I'd love the company. Tom can sleep on the couch, if he doesn't mind," Alma said.

"Well, if you're absolutely certain, we wouldn't be putting you out," Joan said.

"Nonsense, it's all settled. I'd be glad to have you stay with me and there's plenty of space for the three of us," Alma replied.

"My name is on the Hertz rental agreement, and Joan's name is on the hostel lease. I'll move our things out of the hostel and get rid of the rental car so we won't be so easy to find after this," I said.

"I'll have Rob take care of getting another leased car in his name for you," Alma said. "Then it can't be traced back to you. He can pick you up at the car rental place, and you can drive to my apartment after."

"Well, that takes care of that part. When the doctor shows up this morning, I'll have to find out if I can get out of here today," Joan said.

"This sounds like déjà vu all over again. Didn't we just go through this back in the Berkshire Medical Center when you insisted I should stay in the hospital until I was back on my feet again?" I said.

"That was you and this is me. Totally different rules apply as far as I'm concerned," Joan said, trying her best to force a smile on her face.

"You women always seem to have a double standard for other people. It's kinda like the toilet seat thing. Why can't you women leave the seat up for us guys instead when you finish?" I asked.

"The way you two bicker back and forth, you sound like an old married couple. I'll go see if I can get in touch with Rob to make arrangements for another rental car while you're waiting for the doctor to show up," Alma said as she picked up her purse and blew Joan a kiss while walking out the door.

"Do you suppose that could be true?" Joan asked.

"What could be true?" I asked, puzzled.

"That we're starting to behave like an old married couple?"

"I don't think so, but would that bother you if it were the case?"

"No, but as a matter of fact, I kind of like the thought. I've been on my own for my whole life. It would be nice to belong to someone and have them belong to me for a change. It's like that old Chinese expression that you become responsible for a person if you save their life. Since we've each saved the other on this assignment, we should be responsible for one another from now on."

"Joan, I was thinking about that after I was so full of rage at the creep who beat you up. I just wanted to tear him limb from limb without thinking about the consequences. I was so irrational that I couldn't think straight.

"When this relationship started to develop between us, I never envisioned that I could begin to care for you as deeply as I do in such a short period of time. I don't know what to think about us being able to work together anymore if I can't control my emotions on the job."

"We'll have to finish this discussion some other time. That herd of white coats I see in the hall look like they're on the way to this room."

Joan was right. The doctor was making grand rounds with his staff and medical students. They all crowded around Joan's bed. It seemed strange that Joan's arguments for immediate release from the hospital sounded almost verbatim what I had said to Dr. Broz when I was a patient. This doctor was no happier than mine was about an early release, but he reluctantly agreed to sign the papers for Joan to leave right away.

32

Alma returned from making arrangements with Rob to get me a newly leased car that couldn't be traced to Joan or me. She said she would get her car from the parking lot and pull up to the front door. I waited to go down in the elevator with Joan as she was being pushed in a wheelchair by a nurse's aide.

We stopped briefly at the administrative office for Joan to sign the paperwork to attest she would be responsible for payments not made by the insurance. Since she was still woozy from the pain killers, I helped steady her in the chair while she signed. Outside the lobby, Alma was approaching the entrance as I held the door open. Once we had Joan seated in the car, Alma went back around the car to get in the driver's seat.

Out of habit, Joan gave me a kiss on the cheek as I leaned in to fasten her seat belt. I'm sure that Alma must have noticed, but she didn't say anything. I said good-bye, wished them a safe trip and closed the door.

I had informed Alma it would take me about an hour to pack all our things and check out of the hostel so I could meet Rob at the Hertz car rental counter inside the Zurich airport.

I hoped the Asians hadn't noticed the Hertz decal on our rental car when they kidnapped Joan, but I stayed off the main roads and took frequent turns to make certain I wasn't being followed to the airport.

I quickly checked the rental back in the remote Hertz parking and dragged our two bags to the Avis office in the next lot. Even though my shoulder felt better, I was glad our luggage had wheels. I told the Avis people that I would be meeting someone at their booth shortly. They were kind enough to allow me to store the two suitcases while I went to find him.

I went inside to the baggage claim area and stood in a corner of the Europcar rental area behind an artificial ficus tree to watch the Hertz counter for Rob. Sure enough, he was right on time. I waved at him to get his attention, and he followed me at a distance out the side door.

Rob was parked at the curb section designated for arriving passenger loading, so we had to make a loop of the airport to pick up the luggage in the Avis parking lot field office. Soon enough, we had cleared the airport exit and were satisfied we didn't have anyone tailing us. Then Rob inquired how Joan was doing.

"She was man-handled pretty bad so she's really sore. Fortunately there was nothing broken. Alma took her home today to her apartment in Lucerne," I said. "Did they learn anything from the guy we caught at the cottage?"

"Joan was right. He is Chinese. We found out his name is Wu Chen from his prints on file at Interpol. They've been looking for him for years. He's a mercenary who mostly did work for the North Koreans. So far, he hasn't said much, but he was last known to be in Hong Kong," Rob said.

"Did they figure out who the other one was?" I asked.

"Based on the fingerprints left at the cottage, his partner is Li Yang who is from a different area in China. Apparently they have worked in Europe together before contracting with North Korea. We still don't know who their contact is or what the details of their assignments are though."

"Is there any news from Alex yet on improvements in Peter Pickering's condition?" I asked.

"Peter has been progressing in starts and stops. He has had flashbacks of being attacked, but then he can't tie them to any other events before or after that. The doctors said it'll probably take a lot of time before he can connect all the dots of what happened to him," Rob said.

Rob proceeded to a car rental agency on Gatenhofstrasse in Zurich downtown. Pulling up to the curb in front, he said, "You take this car, and I'll rent another one. The gas tank is full. I'll give you a call tomorrow, and we can decide where we can go from here. Did Alma give you instructions on how to get to her apartment?"

"Yes, she did. Thank you for everything. We'll see you tomorrow."

The early afternoon traffic was light, and I soon arrived at Alma's apartment. She greeted me at the door wearing a pair of oven mitts. "Are you expecting snow, or are your hands just cold?" I asked.

"If you must know, I was just about to take a pasta casserole out of the oven for dinner. Joan looked like she could use a little nourishment that didn't require much chewing after her ordeal yesterday," Alma said. "If you'd like to make yourself useful, you can remove the cork on the bottle of liebfraumilch that's chilling in the ice bucket. The corkscrew is on the counter next to the stove.

Joan was already seated at the table, which was set for three. I wrapped the bottle in a napkin and proceeded with the uncorking. "You're looking somewhat better this afternoon," I said to Joan.

"Alma left me undisturbed so I could have a long nap. I didn't sleep much, but the rest seemed to help a lot," Joan said quietly with a weak smile.

Since Joan still looked fatigued, Alma and I ended up talking about anything except for the case we were working on. It seemed we had an unspoken agreement to not talk shop in front of Joan for the duration of the evening.

When we finished dinner and a strudel with a combination of at three different fruits, I complimented Alma on the delicious meal and helped her clean the kitchen. After watching the world news in English on BBC, Alma suggested that we turn in after the last two busy days. Since Joan really needed the rest, I wholeheartedly agreed. They said good night and retired to their respective bedrooms.

I had turned off the light in the living room and reclined on the couch for what seemed to be an eternity but just couldn't get to sleep thinking about Joan. Suddenly I heard a bang and moan. I quickly grabbed my gun and switched on the light. Joan was standing in front of me in her nightgown, rubbing her big toe. She signaled to me that I should follow her into her bedroom so I shut off the light.

Once she closed the door, I whispered, "What are you doing? Alma is in the next room, and you are supposed to be getting bed rest."

"I was going nuts. I couldn't get to sleep last night without you, and it wasn't happening tonight either. I need to be close to you," she whispered. "Come lay on the bed with me. If we can cuddle, then maybe I can finally get some sleep. I'm sooo tired and desperately need to rest."

"Joan, this is crazy. If word gets back to Alex, this would end our chances of working and being together. You know the CIA has a strict no fraternization policy."

"I don't care. I miss you so much, and I really have to get some sleep. I can't do it without you next to me."

"Okay, maybe for a little while, but I have to get back to the couch before Alma wakes up in the morning," I said as she snuggled up to me on the bed.

33

I woke to see the bright sun streaming in through the edges of the translucent window shade. My watch said it was a little after six in the morning. Without waking her, I managed to carefully nudge Joan's arm and leg off me as I slid down to the floor. Being as quiet as possible in opening and closing the bedroom door, I returned to the couch in the living room.

I must have made more noise than I thought. Immediately after closing my eyes, I heard a little creaking sound. I ignored it until I felt a warm kiss being planted on my forehead. Looking up, I was surprised to see Alma standing like a genie in an akimbo pose in front of the sofa with a silly grin on her face.

"Your secret is safe with me," she whispered and then winked at me.

"What are you talking about?" I asked.

"You know very well I'm talking about you and Joan. I got up for a drink of water in the middle of the night, and you weren't on the couch. I saw how she gave you a kiss in the car when she was still only half conscious. I've also seen how the two of you look at each other. You're so much more than just partners. I couldn't possibly have missed the violent look of rage in your eyes when you tackled that Chinese guy who beat up Joan."

"Our feelings for each other kind of snuck up on us. It just gradually happened after spending so much time together. We're trying to figure out what it all means. She said she couldn't get to sleep without me being next to her, so we cuddled."

"It must have worked. I didn't hear anything the rest of the night. I happen to think it's sweet. Perhaps one day I'll find someone who cares that much about me. Don't worry, I won't tell anybody. If you're worried about Rob slipping up at some point, he doesn't have to know. It can just be kept between the three of us."

"That makes sense to me," I said. "I'll let Joan know you're in on our little secret later."

"You'll do no such thing, Tom Powers. After the beating Joan was subjected to when she was being interrogated, she needs all the comforting she can get. You are going to march right back in there. Then you'd better snuggle up to her and whisper sweet nothings in her ear until she has a smile on her face or I won't be happy with you either. I can throw breakfast together whenever you two decide to get up. Now get your butt next to hers before she realizes you're gone."

"Yes, ma'am," I said. Returning to the bedroom, I tried to slide under the covers again without disturbing Joan.

"Tom, what are you doing in here again? You'd better get back to the couch before Alma wakes up," Joan said.

"It's too late. She already knows. Alma figured out that there was something going on between us. She saw you kiss me in the car while you were still half out of it. She doesn't have a problem with us being a couple. We just won't tell Rob," I said.

"Mmmm, in that case, come here and kiss me," she said, pulling me closer.

"Aren't your lips too sore for that?" I asked.

"I think they're getting better. Pucker up and we'll find out for sure."

Breaking our lip lock a few minutes later, I said, "This isn't going to work. I want you too much, and you are in no shape for that kind of activity yet."

"How will we know unless we try that too?" she said, grinning.

"No way, Jose, just cuddle up and enjoy us being together for a while. Alma said she'd hold off breakfast until we are ready to come out and join her. Just put your head on my shoulder and try to get back to sleep. You need all the rest you can get for the time being."

"Okay, but I'm going to be disappointed. I'm spoiled and can't get enough of you." Joan rolled toward me with her head in the crook of my arm, moaned contentedly, and soon, was fast asleep.

Meanwhile I had so many things on my mind that I just couldn't sleep. After staring at the ceiling for the longest time, I vacillated from being thrilled about being with Joan to thinking this was all wrong for her. Here she was at the start of her career and a life that could involve having children of her own. As wonderful as the prospect of spending the rest of my life with Joan seemed to be, it felt as if she would be short changed by not finding someone closer to her own age and with the same lifetime goals.

I managed to slide out of bed again without waking her. Alma looked surprised to see me so soon, but I assured her that Joan was sound asleep, getting the rest she desperately needed.

By the time we were having our second cup of coffee, Joan walked into the living room, looking much improved over the night before. Maybe it was mostly due to the fact that she was more rested today. "What's going on?" she asked, seeing the two of us sitting in the middle of the room.

"We were just discussing breakfast. I have eggs, cereal, and pancake mix. What would you like?" Alma asked.

"I'm starving after not eating much for the last three days. If it's not too much trouble, I think I could handle scrambled eggs and some toast if I could dunk it in coffee," Joan said as she appeared to be trying her best to manage a smile through the pain.

"No problem, how about you, Tom?" Alma said.

"Cold cereal and more coffee would be great," I said.

Alma had everything she needed already set out on the table and counter. She placed the milk and cereal down in front of me. After starting a fresh pot of coffee, she proceeded to scramble the eggs and toast the bread.

"Rob is going to call this morning and help us decide what we should to do next," I said. "I have copies of all the Pickering and van Rijn invoice documentation with me in my suitcase."

"Up to this point, it looks as though all this is about North Korea wanting to make weapons for themselves and to sell them on the world market," Alma said, looking very domesticated in her frilly apron with her curly Gaelic red hair ablaze in the intense rays of the morning sun bursting through the kitchen window.

"Except we would rather they not do it with the help of American technology that actually works," I said, out of the side of my mouth now full of crunchy cereal. "The United Kingdom and European Union have similar prohibitions to ours on goods which could contribute to North Korea's nuclear efforts, weapons of mass destruction, and ballistic missile programs."

"Well, other than the few Japanese and German goods North Korea imports they seem to prefer American products. The CIA doesn't have a good handle on how much effort the UK and EU are expending on enforcing their bans," Alma said as she set two plates of scrambled eggs and toast on the table. Before sitting down with us, Alma turned on the television to listen to the world news on BBC One.

As the news was finishing up after breakfast, Rob called, so I put him on speaker phone. I told him Alma and Joan were within earshot whereby they immediately hit him with a melodious chorus of, "Good morning, Rob," almost simultaneously.

"Hi, everyone, how are you feeling today, Joan?" Rob inquired.

"Still sore, but I'm almost functional again. Thank you for asking," Joan said with her lips moving with apparently more ease than the day before.

"I was thinking this would be a good time to meet for a face-to-face discussion if Joan is up for it. We've got too many loose pieces of data to try to fit into the puzzle to make sense of it by ourselves," Rob said.

"That sounds like a good idea, Rob. What time can you get here?" I asked.

"It's the middle of the night back in Virginia. I have a conference call scheduled with Alex and his people at 7:00 AM, Langley time. There's a place called *Pizza und Kebab One* on the way. It's a take away pizzeria on Obergrundstrasse. I can pick up a couple of large pizzas and be at Alma's place for a late lunch a little after 2:00 PM," Rob said.

"That would work for us. We can try to sort out the facts we have on hand in the meantime," Alma said.

"It sounds like a plan. We'll see you then, Rob," I said.

While Alma was pouring us each another cup of coffee, I dug out the paperwork I had accumulated on the case. We cleared the kitchen table and started at the beginning to review the case so we could determine what we had learned thus far.

Joan lead off with "We originally became aware of what the North Koreans were up to when we discovered unexploded ordinance on the south side of the demilitarized zone. Many of the components consisted of modified parts from American made automobiles, commercial electronics, industrial equipment, and appliances.

"We found serial numbers that could be traced back to Peter Pickering's Three P distribution Company. He was enlisted to help the CIA ascertain how these components were finding their way to North Korea. Then we lost contact with Peter."

"That's when Monique Pickering came into my office seeking my help to find Peter. She did receive a threat in the mail that was posted locally. Since I knew Alex, I called him at the CIA for his assistance. It turned out that Peter had been hit on the head and left for dead," I said. "Alex's people in Germany were able to confirm his identity and ferry him back to the states on a medevac flight."

"Peter was in a coma when Alex introduced me to Tom and said we'd be working together," Joan said. "We interrupted a break-in at Peter's house in the Berkshires where Tom was shot, by a woman or small man who escaped."

"The only clues we had led us to a safe deposit box in Berkshire Bank and subsequently another one at the United Bank of Switzerland in Zurich. That's when we found Peter's journal and the invoices for the shipments to Taiwan," I said.

"We interrupted another break-in at van Rijn's Swiss office. We were too late to save the Dutchman, but Tom shot one of the North Korean spies. We did manage to capture the other one alive," Joan said. "Then we found the Dutchman's briefcase hidden in his home in Holland after it was ransacked. From that, we were able to determine he was also ordering components direct from eleven other suppliers in the States."

"Except for the ghost story that might have forewarned me about Joan's impending kidnapping, that brings us up to date. Apparently, that was just a figment of my imagination when I was half asleep anyway. We still have to put all these pieces together to figure out how to stop what the North Koreans are trying to do," I said. "Now we need to see what Rob learned from his conference call today and determine how that helps us."

34

As promised, Rob showed up with a couple of large, steaming, hot, deep-dish pizzas and two cold bottles of diet Pepsi. Fortunately, we saw him pull up to the curb and somehow manage to close the car door with his elbow to make it to the porch in one trip. How he expected to ring the doorbell carrying all of that is beyond me. I opened the door while Joan grabbed the pizzas as they started to tip off his open palm. That action shifted his balance, but Alma was sufficiently alert to catch the two-liter colas from his other hand.

Rob immediately bowed from the waist and said with a big grin. "Thank you, thank you very much. For my next trick, I plan to defy gravity."

"Before you start to levitate by inflating your already swelled head, you've got three hungry people here who haven't had a bite to eat since breakfast," Alma said. "We left no stone unturned in assembling a list of the elements that comprise our investigative efforts thus far. Yet we have diligently awaited any knowledge you may have managed to glean from your telephone conference call today to complete the overall composite picture. Let's put first things first, however. The table has been cleared and set. Let's eat."

"I'll second that motion," Joan said. "I'm starved."

"That sounds like it's a good sign your recovery is going well, partner. Hopefully that means you're starting to feel better," I said. "The swelling around your eye finally seems to be going down a little bit too."

"Come to think about it, I'm not really quite as sore today as I was yesterday," Joan said, already seated at the table and extracting a pizza slice with everything on it. "Small movements aren't quite as much an adventure into severe pain as they were yesterday."

"That's great news," Alma said, bringing four glasses with ice cubes to the table.

"By the way, thank you for leaving off the anchovies, Rob," Joan said, making a face.

"Okay Rob, so what's new and exciting at Langley that we need to know about?" I asked once everyone was seated and had a piece of pizza.

Rob held up his left index finger after he had just stuffed the rest of his first piece in his mouth. Sipping from his glass of Pepsi to help wash it down, he said, "Hey, don't be in such a rush. I didn't have lunch yet either. I did hear a new name today. There were rumors about the head of North Korea's spy organization with a code name of Imugi, but I thought somebody just made that name up. Interpol found his prints at the Dutchman's house in Ede."

"I recall a story about him back when I was in the service. If it was true, it's hard to believe that he's still around and has managed to elude capture all these years. Why would he be in Europe himself instead of getting one of his henchmen to do whatever he was trying to accomplish?" I asked.

"From what I've heard, he's totally hands on, especially when he's displeased with his minions who couldn't get the job done," Rob said, taking another slice and refilling his glass with cola.

"What does Imugi translate to in English?" I asked.

"His name might reflect his attitude and approach to his assignments. He bides his time, but ultimately, he's totally intent on fulfilling all of the goals he set for himself for each and every one of his missions," Rob said. "I looked it up. An Imugi (Ee-Moo-Gi) is a mythical hornless creature native to Korea that resembles a giant python or serpent that lives in water or caves. These proto-dragons must survive for one thousand years if they aspire to become full-fledged dragons. The belief is that they are close relatives of dragons and must pass three tests of courage before they are transformed to actual dragons with wings and feet."

"So do we think Imugi wants to be promoted to a higher office in the North Korean political scheme of pecking order, or what?" I asked.

"Langley didn't know. They were surprised he was in this region and didn't know what his relationship with the Chinese mercenaries was," Rob said.

"Did they manage to get any information from Wu Chen on where Li Yang might have gone after he left the cottage?" Joan asked, pulling a hot piece of pepperoni off her pizza and shaking the melted cheese from her fingertips. "Burns my lips."

"No, not yet, but I suspect they will try drugs or hypnotism to coax it out of Chen. They found a psychiatrist who has used hypnotism successfully for interrogation. He is fluent in Mandarin and English, but Chen speaks a dialect of Wu from Shanghai called Shanghainese. They are checking out all the local universities for a translator, but less than 6 percent of the Chinese population can speak the Wu dialect," Rob said. "They will let us know if and when they make any progress with him."

"Has there been any improvement in Peter's condition?" I asked.

"The good news was that Peter has continued to make good progress and may ultimately be on the road to achieving a complete recovery. His memory may be fuzzy, but he still improves from one day to the next. Monique has been determined to attend to his every need on an ongoing basis.

She has been quizzing him on their travels and acquaintances to recapture the missing pieces of the man he once was.

"Your cousin Janyce went up to the Pickering house in the Berkshires and found several photograph albums that weren't destroyed when the place was ransacked."

"Monique is relentless in working with him steadily. She keeps going over and over the photos with Peter of their past together because it seems to be helping to restore his memory a little bit at a time," Rob said.

"Has he remembered anything else?" I asked.

"He said he was attacked by a couple of Asian guys when he was in Basel on his way to an appointment with Herr Schneider at Electronikindustrie. He heard them talking after they hit him on the head before they threw him into the trunk of his car. He said he was pretty groggy after being clobbered, but thinks one was named Chen and the other Yang," Rob said.

"That tells us Li and Imugi might be the only other perps we have to look for. That's good information. That also means Li Yang had to be fluent in the Wu dialect if he could converse with Chen. Was Peter able to provide any other details?" I asked.

"None about his abduction yet, but he is making great strides in recovering both his long- and short-term memory. Monique told Alex that his sense of humor is starting to return, along with recapturing certain other traits of his personality," Rob said.

"We have to sort this out and put it all in perspective," Joan said. "Peter was clobbered by the Chinese mercenaries in Basel before the North Korean spies killed the Dutchman and tried to destroy his files in Zurich. That says both Asian assassin teams were in Switzerland at the same time, but we don't know what Imugi was looking for at van Rijn's house in Holland."

"Joan brings up an interesting point," I said. "The North Koreans don't know that the briefcase we found hidden at the Dutchman's house had invoices from his eleven suppliers in the United States. What does the CIA plan to do to stop those distributors and the Lotus Trading Company in Taipei?"

"Funny thing you should bring it up. The simple answer is, *nothing at all*," Rob said.

"Nothing? How can you say that? Joan was kidnapped, and we both came close to being killed. You mean to say we did all that for naught?" I demanded.

"Relax, Tom, I was saving the best for last. We've got a plan. It will appear to the North Koreans as though we don't know what they are doing. They will be under the impression we are not taking any action against them. As far as they are concerned, they will believe their covert actions were successful in covering up their operations," Rob said.

"So what exactly will we be doing? Alma asked, incredulously.

"When contacted, the eleven sources in the States will continue to ship to Taiwan exactly the finished assemblies ordered. What the North Koreans won't know is that all the circuitry in the products shipped will have undersized conductors. They will be sufficiently functional to only pass initial testing. Unfortunately for Kim Jong-un, the junction temperatures in the circuit boards will rise to the point of overheating when full field loads are applied after they have been incorporated into North Korean weapon systems," Rob said.

"Sounds like a great plan to me. *Dear Leader* will be really irritated with his people, especially if they can't tell the difference between the earlier prototype weapons and the modified versions," Joan said.

"Okay, what will we be doing in the meantime then?' I asked.

"We still have to capture Li Yang and see if we can get the location of Imugi out of Wu Chen," Rob said.

"Then there's the matter of figuring out who tried to take a shot at me in Massachusetts and sent the threatening letter to Monique," Joan said.

"Oh, I'm glad you brought that up. The CIA had finally worn down Kang Sang-hee to the point where she confessed to lying about the degree of her involvement in the North Korean spy agency. Sang-hee was the one who sent the threatening letter to Monique, ransacked the Pickering home in the Berkshires, and shot Tom before she returned to Zurich. Since she was the only agent in the States, it suggests the Pickerings could have no problems returning home upon Peter's released from the hospital in Bethesda," Rob said.

"That is good news," I said.

"Well, I guess we've covered all the bases," Rob said as he got up to leave. "Let me know if you learn anything more. I'll keep you posted on what's happening at headquarters." Rob returned to the table to grab another slice of pizza. "One for the road."

Following up on loose ends in our investigation that need to be addressed, I called Cap. Annitti at Interpol. "Good afternoon, Vito. This is Tom Powers. Have you had any luck in finding out where is a likely place to look for Imugi, the North Korean super spy?" I asked.

"*Buongiorno*, Tomaso. We have not managed to pin down his location yet, but we heard a rumor from an informant that he might be at the University of Bern. This is a continuation of the Asian trend of enrolling students who will eventually gain access to the laboratories and management positions in both academia and the business world."

"You mean that North Korea has the patience to wait for years to plant moles in these organizations before they see any results from their efforts?" I asked.

"They have been at it for over fifty years. This way it is much easier for them to launch cyber attacks from the insides of those organizations. We suspect he might be posing as a father figure for North Korean students in an off campus housing facility. That would provide direct access to the work being done by Korean graduate students being paid by industrially funded grants. These firms do not seem to realize that they are supplying their technology directly to the North Koreans who want to use it for conversion into weapons of mass destruction.

"We should get together and review what we have learned to…how do you Americans say… avoid duplication of effort. I happen to be open for tomorrow. Perhaps we could meet."

"I'd like to include my partner Joan, but she is recovering from the beating she took when she was kidnapped."

"To make it easier on her, I could meet you halfway. There is a restaurant called Voile d'Or Café on the hill above Lake Geneva. It is in a little village of Lausanne called Vidy. The address is avenue e. -Jaques Dalcroze 9. I could meet you there for coffee sometime after 11:00 AM."

"That would be great, Vito, *grazie*. I look forward to finally meeting you in person. Ciao, my friend."

35

"Tom, Tom, wake up, it's five thirty in the morning. Alma will be getting up soon so you'd better get going if you want to use the bathroom before breakfast," Joan said. "You said we have to meet Vito in Lausanne in a few hours."

"Okay already, I'm getting up. Good morning, sweetheart, I'll see you at breakfast in a little while," I said, giving her a peck on the cheek before I hurried to stand in front of a razor and hop into the shower.

I dashed into the bedroom to get dressed. When we popped out of the bedroom, Alma was already busy in the kitchen.

"Well, hello there, you two lovebirds. Your timing couldn't be better. Breakfast is almost ready," Alma said.

"Bonjour right back at you," Joan said, beaming her megawatt smile. "Tom told me you are in on our little secret.

That makes everything a lot easier. All of this is new for both of us, so we have no idea where this is going to lead. We're just feeling our way along as we go, if you'll pardon the expression."

"I happen to think it's terrific that you two have something more than work to share together, what with all the stress we're under in trying make the world a safer place," Alma said.

"Everything smells great, Alma. Is there anything I can do to help?" I asked.

"You're too late, it's all done. Just take a seat at the table while I pour the coffee," Alma said. "By the way, Rob called early this morning. He said Alex has to go testify before Congress today about the information leaks that result in the exploitation of proprietary American technology in Asia."

"Does anyone think these meetings will achieve anything positive in terms of accomplishments? Congress can't seem to agree on anything or decide on what action to take," Joan said. "Maybe things will change with the new Republican majority in both houses now though."

"Alex seems to take the approach of keeping them informed on a broad brush basis, but not filling them in on any of the specific details or minutiae. That way they can't try to micromanage and screw everything up. We only want them to approve sufficient funding for us to get our job done without any interference on their part. Then our senators and representatives will feel they are doing something useful," Alma said.

"Did they manage to contact all of the US manufacturers who were supplying the Dutchman with components destined for shipment to Taiwan?" I asked.

"Yeah, the CIA convinced a freight forwarding agent in Barcelona he could get the Lotus Trading business if he offered an extra savings by shipping through South America to reduce the tax bite. He already has placed the initial orders in the US for goods destined for North Korea at much larger quantities than ever before." Then Alma paused to ask, "Would anyone like more coffee?"

"No, thank you. I couldn't handle a third cup, but it was very good," Joan replied. "Thank you for breakfast, but we have to get on the way if we are to meet Vito in three hours."

I slid behind the wheel of the rental car and looked over at Joan. "Are you doing okay?"

"I'm fine. I'm feeling much better today, thank you."

"Reaching for her hand to give it a little squeeze, I said, "I'd better pull into the petrol station to top off the tank before we get going. That one priced at 1.80 Swiss francs per liter equates to about 7.50 a gallon in US dollars. It probably would be significantly cheaper down the road, but we can't take a chance of running out on the highway."

"I'll program the GPS while you are taking care of filling up the tank," Joan said.

"Okay we're fueled, belted, and headlighted, so I guess we're ready to get on the autobahn. It does seem strange that they require the use of headlights over here, day and night. Maybe they have invested heavily into the Philips lightbulb manufacturing plants in the Netherlands.

"I'm glad Rob has cruise control on this rental. I'll set it a little above 120 kilometers per hour once we get underway. You can check the rearview mirror from time to time to see if anyone seems to be following us," I said as I returned to the driver's seat.

After a while on the motorway, Joan leaned to one side and put her head on my shoulder. It wasn't long before she drifted off to sleep. I guess it'll be a while until she gets back up to speed and is acting like her old energetic self again. Meanwhile I was reviewing everything in my mind we had talked about yesterday with Alma and Rob. There seemed to be something missing we didn't address, but I just couldn't put my finger on what that might be.

Not coming up with any solutions to predict what else we could do with the problems posed by North Korea, my thoughts went back to this young beauty at my side. She has everything I could want in a woman. She is vivacious, funny, intelligent, caring, and talented. Gee, I just made her sound like she could qualify to become a girl scout.

Unfortunately I still had the overwhelming feeling that she would be getting the short end of the stick with me as a potential partner for life. Even ignoring the age difference, it just seems that she could do a lot better than what I have to offer her. Maybe I just wasn't cut out to be husband or father material. Besides having been through the mill and back, I never was housebroken and probably wouldn't be trainable in that regard. I didn't seem to be able to reach any conclusions on that front either before Joan started to stir. It was then I noticed a sign that said we were approaching Bern.

"Oh, I'm sorry. I must have dozed off. What time is it?" she asked.

"It's a little after 9:00 AM, we're halfway there. Would you like to stop for a cup of coffee?"

"Yeah, I could use a coffee and make a potty stop while I'm at it."

"I'll pull off the highway the first chance I get then. It wouldn't hurt for me to get out and stretch a little too. I've been watching, but I haven't seen anyone that appears to be following us. Because I'm only doing a little over the speed limit, it seems that everyone is passing us like were standing still."

"I can take a turn driving if you don't think we'd get there too soon," she said with a broad grin.

"Only if you feel like you're up to it," I said, trying to ignore the dig about my driving. "Just remember, we're trying to keep a low profile and don't need any speeding tickets."

"No problem. I'm not hurting as much today so I can pay attention to what I'm doing."

I pulled off the expressway and rounded up a couple of coffees while she went to the little fraulein's room. Joan looked relieved and refreshed as she pulled back onto the highway. My shoulder had healed, but it did feel good not to have to hold the steering wheel. Maybe I should start to do exercises to get the shoulder muscles back into shape.

36

Winding our way up the hill to the village of Vidy in Lausanne, which overlooked Lake Geneva, we located the Voile d'Or Café. There was only one customer sitting outside under the green and white striped awning at one of the tables with the checkered tablecloths flapping in the gentle breeze.

From a sitting position while sipping from a demitasse cup, he appeared to be slight of stature. The wavy jet-black hair and full mustache lent him a sort of movie-star quality. Joan pulled in to park, and I walked over to verify it was Vito since we had only talked over the phone up to this point.

After confirming he was in fact Capt. Annitti of Interpol, I signaled to Joan to join us. Following introductions, he explained that this was one of his favorite cafes because their espresso was comparable to what he was accustomed to drinking in Italy. Vito claimed the espressos made in his region of France just did not have sufficient body to be worth the bother.

Apparently Joan wasn't any fonder of espresso than I was, so we both ordered regular coffee with croissants and cheese. I was pleased to find their drip coffee tasted more like it was from Dunkin' Donuts rather than Starbucks. Supposedly it has something to do with the Arabica beans grown in the Latin American soil and climate combined with their special roasting process.

After being served, we provided a full update to Vito on what we had learned since our last series of telephone discussions. I also told him that interrogation of Wu Chen suggested possible hiding places of his partner Li Yang. I added that further questioning of Kang Sang-hee revealed she was the one who shot me in the United States and mailed the threatening letter to Monique Pickering.

Joan and I were careful to omit any discussions on the CIA's planned attempt to sabotage North Korea's efforts to become a credible weapons supplier on the open market for terrorists and rogue nations. Vito was well aware that North Korea had already sullied their reputation for repair and rework of Russian made weapons for the third world countries.

Vito thanked us for sharing the information saying that many officials from other countries are not as willing to offer useful data on a timely basis. After a long and deliberate pause, he cautiously looked to the left and right as if his head was on a swivel. At last he told us that Interpol suspected North Korea either had a mole at Interpol or had successfully launched a cyber attack to hack their computer systems. Among other things, every time Interpol had a lead on a possible Imugi location, he would disappear immediately before they arrived.

In a very quiet voice, he almost whispered that Li Yang had been seen in the outskirts of Basel. We had to lean forward and listen carefully in order to hear him. Interpol assumed Imugi was displeased with Li and Wu's failure to obtain meaningful information in the course of Joan's kidnapping. At least he never tolerated incompetence from subordinates or his mercenaries in the past, so Imugi may show up in that area as well.

Vito handed me a slip of paper that narrowed down what they thought was Li's location within a few blocks in Basel based on calls from his cell phone. It also had Li Yang's cell phone number. He figured the CIA had better resources available than Interpol to follow up these leads.

We thanked Vito and told him we'd keep him posted on our progress. As we stood to leave, he gestured to the waitress and pointed to his espresso cup for a refill.

Since it was my turn to drive, Joan reset the GPS again. I was glad she liked to do that sort of thing. Messing with those gadgets was never one of my favorite pastimes. All these modern electronic contraptions that come out now seem to be made for fingers much smaller than mine. Every time I try to use one, more than one function at a time is hit and I have to start the process all over again. In the future, we may have to hire smaller people just to use them. I wonder if there's a strategic diet application to reduce the size of one's fingers? That must be why women keep their fingernails long and sharpened.

We waved good-bye to Vito as we drove off. Because we were no longer looking for the café as we started back, we had a chance to observe the sailboats below as we worked our way down the hill. The boats bobbed up and down as they zipped over the wind driven whitecaps on Lake Geneva in the sunshine. They seemed to be playfully tacking back and forth to catch the wind. I made a mental note that perhaps we could return to try a little sailing if we ever get a chance to vacation in this area together.

Joan leaned in my direction to snuggle up as close as the seat belt would allow, but would watch the rear view mirrors from time to time to make certain we were not being followed. As I drove up to the higher elevations in the Alps we had to keep swallowing to equalize the pressure on our inner ears. Fortunately, Joan had a pack of gum which seemed to provide some relief.

Once we were acclimated to the reduced pressure at the "rooftop of Europe" (as the taller Alps in Switzerland are sometimes called), Joan stretched out across the seat and rested her head in my lap as she took a nap. She probably didn't realize how much of a distraction this was when I was trying to concentrate on the driving in the mountainous terrain with all the road curves involved, in addition to hers.

When we were about halfway back, I pulled off the autobahn, and we stopped for a late lunch in a small village. It appeared Joan was almost back to being her old self with her aggressive driving style when she took her turn behind the wheel once again. While I was trying to make certain we were not being followed, I found myself stepping on the floor panel when I felt someone should be applying the brakes at those speeds going downhill and around the curves. If Joan noticed the actions of my feet, she was doing an exceptional job of ignoring them.

When we returned to Alma's apartment, we found a note addressed to us on the kitchen table. She said she had run out on a few errands but would return before dark.

Joan indicated that she was a little tired after our long day of driving and would try to take a little nap to rest up. I told her I would give Alex a call to update him on what we had discussed with Interpol.

Once Joan retired to the bedroom and closed the door, I put a call through to Langley. In no time at all, the voice with the smile in it was on the other end of the line and acted as if we were old friends. When I asked for Alex, she said he was in a Middle East status report meeting with the Department of State, but she'd have him call as soon as he was available.

37

I was lost in my thoughts concerning our assignment in regards to North Korea interspersed with daydreams of how wonderful I feel when I'm with Joan. I was making absolutely no forward progress in resolving either predicament when my cell phone rang. "Hi, Tom, this is Alex."

"I heard you were in the middle of testifying before the joint sessions of Congress on the drains of American technology to Asia. When I called, Susan said you were getting the Department of State squared away on the crises in the Middle East. What's up with that anyway?"

"Apparently I'm one of the few old timers with enough experience on how the Asian exploitation of US technology started, so I drew the short straw for testifying. It doesn't matter that the CIA is trying to keep a lid on the potential powder keg in the Middle East. So what did you learn from your meeting with Interpol?" Alex asked.

I filled Alex in on what Captain Annitti's assessment of North Korea's position was. That included the fact that he thought they either had a mole in Interpol or their computers were being hacked. Alex's lack of reaction on the phone suggested he wasn't surprised that Imugi might try to kill one of his hired henchmen who couldn't get the job done.

He said he had to leave immediately for his assignment as director of the CIA's Middle East Branch to replace his predecessor who was killed in a Baghdad explosion. Rob will be promoted to Acting CIA director of the European Operations to replace him. Alma will be notified shortly about who her new partner will be as soon as the selection process is completed and the transfer papers can be processed.

Alex said he had to run but told me to let him know if we need any assistance. He added that he'd try his best to keep in touch to see if he could help our progress.

Almost immediately after I hung up with Alex, my phone rang again. "Hi, Tom, this is Janyce. Is this a good time for you to talk?"

"No problem, cuz. I just got back from a field trip. What's up with you?"

"I know you're probably busy as all get out, but I just got a call from Kathy McClellan. You must remember when you put her ex-husband in jail after he beat her up and tried to kill her."

"Yeah, I remember that, only too well. What's going on?" I said.

"Kathy's desperate and doesn't know what to do since Evan was released early from prison on probation. She had another restraining order put out on him, but it hasn't done any good. He's still been stalking her and calling continuously with threats at all hours of the night anyway. Since the cops haven't been able to catch him at it, she thinks you're the only one that can help. Evan again threatened to kill her and take the kids too. She's scared to death and afraid to leave the house or let the kids out of her sight."

"Well, I don't know what I can do right now. There have been some recent developments here so we might be switching people around. Things have become complicated with my partner on this case too."

"Uh-oh, I thought I sensed you two were beginning to bond when you were back here. She did seem to be exceptionally protective of you," Janyce said with a hint of a chuckle.

"Janyce, I had just taken a bullet that was meant for her. Of course she was grateful. At that time, we were just watching out for each other like all partners do. Since then, she has saved my life too. I'm worried that now she wants a lot more than that. I keep telling her I'm too old for her, and she could do a lot better than what I have to offer," I said.

"From where I sit, it sounds like it has already become serious."

"Not only that, but her dad doesn't want her dating any white guys," I said. "He worries that if he has biracial grandkids, they won't be accepted by either white or black people. I'm not sure where she stands on having children, but both my kids will be finishing up school soon. I'm reasonably certain that I don't want to start all over again with raising a family."

"Well, I hope it works out for the two of you. In the meantime, what can I tell Kathy? She's beside herself and doesn't know which way to turn," Janyce said.

"We're in the middle of redrawing our revised action plan based on what's happened so far. You can tell Kathy to hang in there, and I'll try to get back to her in the next day or two. Just be careful you don't promise her anything on my behalf. I might not be able to help her out."

"What is she supposed to do until then?" Janyce asked in a frustrated tone of voice.

"See if you and Jerry can't take turns dropping by to keep an eye on her."

"I know it's a lot to ask of you when you're busy over there, but anything you can do to help her out will be fully appreciated," Janyce said.

"I'll see if I can't figure something out to resolve the situation or refer her to someone else who can. Take care of yourself, cuz."

My head was spinning after I hung up, trying to determine how I could help the CIA on this case and make arrangements to provide protection for Kathy at the same time. On top of that, what about Joan? I can't let her continue thinking we might have a future together if I'm convinced it's not in her best interest.

I fixed a pot of coffee and was on my second cup mulling things over when Joan woke up and wandered barefoot into the kitchen looking as sexy as all get out. She leaned over my shoulder, gave me a kiss, and asked why I looked so pensive.

I explained that Alex said Rob was the new regional acting director and the CIA would be looking for a replacement partner for Alma. Then I told her about the call from my cousin Janyce while Joan was filling a coffee mug for herself.

"Mmmm," she said as she sipped the hot coffee. "I really needed that nap and this. Thank you for making a pot."

"I needed some too, but it doesn't seem to be helping resolve my dilemma any."

"You might think this is crazy, but what if I were to tell you that I didn't fully appreciate how much I enjoyed working in the field until I started doing it again? Of course, being able to spend all this time with you might have something to do with it."

"Okay, so how does that help me out of the predicament that I'm in?" I asked.

"We're at a point where we need to wait to see if the Alex plan for North Korea works. The only loose element we know about is Imugi. If the lead from Interpol on his whereabouts doesn't pan out, we'll have to find him some other way. So why don't I ask for a transfer to become Alma's new partner here? This could be a trial run for me to see if I really like it and if Langley will be pleased with my performance," Joan said.

"You'd have to be loco to consider staying around here when Imugi and his friends might still be looking for you. I don't want to take a chance on leaving you alone," I said. "You still haven't fully recuperated from the last time they beat you up."

"Tom, the risk comes with the territory. I can take care of myself, especially if I'm aware that they may still be trying to find me. Besides, I'd have Rob and Alma around for backup. When you return from the States, we can decide where we are at and where we want to go from there."

"That's just it. How will I know that you won't get yourself killed while I'm gone?"

"I won't be in any more danger that you will be. I've kind of sensed uneasy vibes still are emanating from you whenever I try to talk to you about our long-term future. I'd miss you a lot, but if you were to take a break for a few weeks to help out your former client, we could see where our relationship stands when you return," Joan said, looking up at me with those gorgeous brown eyes of hers.

"Well you might be right. I don't know who else I could get to solve Kathy McClellan's problem with her ex-husband. I'm still worried about leaving you here in the middle of this mess. I'm also troubled that you could be moving too fast in deciding what your future will be."

"Don't you mean *our* future? I'm already convinced I know how I feel. You're the one dragging his feet," she said with her arms wrapped around my neck.

"It does seem as though we rushed into a relationship too fast. Maybe that's because my marriage and raising the two kids didn't work out very well for me. I still think you might change your mind about starting a family someday. Perhaps we can both examine at our situation in a few weeks down the road from a new perspective. Then we could figure out what we want to do about it from that point," I said.

"Okay, I can't possibly put a positive spin on the fact that we'll be apart that long, but maybe you'll miss me enough to realize that you'll never want to be away from me again," Joan said as she nuzzled my neck with a volley of butterfly kisses that was causing a severe meltdown of any resistance on my part and send a delicious chill down my spine. "I do know it'll seem like the longest three or four weeks of my life so you'd better hurry back to me all in one piece as soon as you can."

38

At an altitude of thirty-five thousand feet, I found myself sitting in a wide body plane that was barely above the cloud cover. I was wracked with guilt having left Joan and Alma at the airport. Alex was glad to have a replacement for Rob that didn't require training. Alma had bonded with Joan and was pleased to have her as a new partner. Other than the fact that I was going away, Joan was thrilled to have a field assignment on a somewhat more permanent basis, even if it was tentative.

Here I was running away from the first woman in years that made me grateful to be alive and anxiously looking forward to every day I could spend with her. I was totally torn between the facts that I was so lucky to have found someone that wonderful yet, at the same time, overwhelmed with the feeling that she was being shortchanged by me. I still couldn't understand what she could possibly see in me or how I could make her half as happy as she makes me.

Then there's the life expectancy thing. Even if I wanted more kids, I probably wouldn't be around long enough to see them graduate or get married. If we were to become a permanent couple now, she'd probably be here on this Earth twice as long as I would be. How is that fair to her?

Somewhere in this argument I was having with myself, I must have dozed off because I heard the "Fasten your seatbelts" announcement and the clunk of the landing gears locking into place as we began our descent into the airspace of the greater New York City metropolitan area. My seat and tray were in their full upright positions as we hit the tarmac hard with an extra bounce due to the higher speed required to compensate for the heavy crosswinds. The angry brakes were screaming and the tires smoking as we gradually reduced speed. It always seemed to me that we wouldn't be able to slow down enough before the end of the runway when we come in that hot. Somehow we were able to turn off the main runway in time to taxi slowly to the designated gate.

Everyone tried to stand in the aisle as soon as the mechanical ding signaled we had come to a complete stop at the boarding ramp for deplaning. I had to get up as well to work the cramps out of my legs from sitting too long. Of course the overhead storage bins were only sufficiently high enough for the vertically challenged to assume a completely erect posture. I had to maneuver into the already crowded aisle to become fully upright myself. I wasn't able to reach for my carry-on luggage until the people between my seat in coach and the exit door had thinned.

Walking down the terminal corridor toward customs, I suddenly felt reconnected. I was back again on my native soil. Extended travel can be a good thing, but there's nothing like home sweet home. I was glad that I didn't have any baggage to claim or purchases to declare as I entered the serpentine line to have my luggage blessed by the government designated agents prior to my liberation from the herd. Turning to the parking and ground transportation area, I encountered the familiar lovely face of my cousin Janyce wearing a big smile.

"Hi, Tom, am I ever glad to see you," she said as she gave me a big hug and a kiss on the cheek. "I've been so worried about leaving Kathy McClellan alone. I didn't know what to do when Jerry or I couldn't be there for her during the times when both of us had to be back at work. A least we could take turns spending the nights with her and the cruisers could drive past her place periodically during the daytime hours."

"Hi, cuz, I've missed you too. I'll see if I can't take up the slack to help put Kathy's ex-husband back behind bars where he belongs. You'd think he'd just leave the area once he got his freedom again instead of hanging around and threatening Kathy," I said. "We just have to catch Evan in the act of harassing her before he hurts her or the kids."

"I hope we can. She's really a sweetheart and doesn't deserve all this abuse and aggravation. Did you have a good flight?"

"There was a little bit of turbulence, but not bad except for a bumpy landing. Is Jerry with Kathy and the kids now?"

"Yeah, I brought your car so you can drop me off at work as soon as we get back. I'm running a little late for my shift, and Jerry has been with her for quite a while," Janyce said. "I put your service revolver and holster in the glove compartment for you."

"Thank you, I feel a little naked when I have to travel without a weapon. No problem dropping you off at the station first. I'll relieve Jerry and Kathy can fill me in on all the blanks so I can figure out how we can stop this idiot before he attacks someone."

The Taconic Parkway only saves fifteen miles compared to I-87, but both routes take a little under three hours. I always preferred the scenic option with the winding roads as long as we didn't run into Bambi or any close relatives in the sparsely populated stretches. At least the traffic was lighter this way. Janyce was happy she didn't have to drive back and we had a chance to discuss everything that happened while I was in Switzerland before she fell asleep.

"Janyce, wake up. We're almost at your precinct."

"What? Oh, I must have drifted off. Sorry, I didn't realize that I was that tired. Fine company I am after your long flight."

"That's perfectly okay. I really appreciate you driving all the way down to New Jersey to pick me up. That saved me sitting in another airport about thirteen hours waiting to change planes," I said. "Do you want to stop for a cup of coffee before we get there?"

"No, I'd better not. My shift starts soon. You should go relieve Jerry, so he can get some sleep. We've both been burning the candle at both ends lately. Just drop me off over there by the side door."

"Thanks again for everything, Janyce. I really appreciate it. Talk to you later."

"I know, Kathy will be relieved and feel safer with you there full time. Good night, Tom," she said as she threw me a kiss, turned on her heels and ran up the steps.

The neighborhood hadn't changed since I was last here a few years ago. I rang the doorbell at Kathy's house. Jerry cautiously opened the door after he checked to verify it was me he could see through the peephole and released the redundant chain lock.

"Tom, great to see you made it back safely. Did you have a good flight?" Jerry said.

"Not bad," I replied as I almost was bowled over when the kids tackled me at the knees screaming, "Uncle Tom."

"Hi, kids," I said, rubbing their heads, surprised that they remembered me since it had been such a long time since they'd last seen me.

"Hi, Tom," Kathy said as she rounded the corner, radiating her usual big smile but looking somewhat haggard and worn out. "I'm so glad you're here. Not that I don't appreciate everything that Jerry and Janyce have done for us in the meantime. You kids go back to the living room and give the grown-ups some space so we can talk."

"Hi, Kathy, I'm glad to see that you've been holding up," I said as I responded to her hug and a kiss on the cheek.

"Tom, I can't begin to tell you how much it means that Janyce and Jerry have been able to help me through the ordeal. It's hard to imagine trying to handle all this stress on my own. I keep thinking Evan will come to the house at any moment," Kathy said.

"Janyce and I have been trying to sneak in and out so Evan would think we've been here all the time," Jerry said.

"Well, now that I can be here around the clock, it probably would be better for my car to disappear. Then I might be able to nab him if he tries to break in," I said. Why don't you go catch up on your sleep and we'll get together with Janyce tomorrow. We'll see if we can figure out how to get him out of Kathy's hair permanently."

"That sounds like a good idea. I'll set the burglar alarm on my way out. Good night, Tom," Jerry said.

As we watched Jerry pull out of the driveway, Kathy turned to me and said, "Would you like a cup of coffee, Tom?"

"I hoped that you would ask. Yes, thank you. It's been a very long day," I said.

We sat at the kitchen table over coffee and cookies while we discussed all the intervening threats, phone calls and drive-bys since Evan was released from prison. My heart went out to Kathy when she reached across the table and put her hand over mine. Looking up, she said, "Tom, I really appreciate you dropping everything to rescue me. I'm sorry you had to come all this way, but maybe I'll finally be able to get a decent night's sleep for a change."

"Don't worry. We'll take care of it. You put the kids to bed and get some rest yourself. We can talk more in the morning."

39

I woke from a semiconscious state of dreamland well short of a deep REM sleep in the recliner while trying to unwind after a long and exhausting day. Once I realized where I was, I sensed a strange overpowering feeling that something was not right. Call it ESP or sixth sense, but this kind of internal warning has happened to me before, and I knew I had to check the situation out. Looking around the living room barely illuminated by a nightlight plugged into a corner wall outlet, nothing seemed to be out of place.

Rising very slowly to minimize making noise, I automatically touched my holster out of habit to make certain my gun was there. Through a tiny gap between the drapes covering the bowed picture window, I could see a dark, mid-sized sedan parked diagonally across the street. The car wasn't there earlier. The dial on my watch said it was almost two in the morning.

A faint glow in the driver's window in an uncupped hand told me someone was taking a drag on a cigarette who had never smoked in a combat zone foxhole. Moving to the adjoining guest room that was unlit, I lifted the bottom slat on the Venetian blind to get a better view through the binoculars. With the slight amount of illumination provided by a sodium vapor streetlight a few houses down the street, I could barely make out what appeared to be the silhouette of a tall male behind the wheel. The amount of amber light was insufficient to determine the color of the car, but it might have been a rusted-out eight- or ten-year-old Toyota.

Extracting the cell phone from my pocket, I punched in Jerry's home number.

"Yeah, what is it? Do you realize what time it is? Who is this?" said a groggy voice on the other end. "Oh, hi, Tom, what's up?

"Sorry to wake you, partner, but there's a dark-colored, old Camry sedan parked across the street from Kathy's house. It might be Evan. Could you have whoever is on duty tonight swing by to see if they can't catch him violating the restraining order? Try to pick someone who won't scare him off. While you're at it, if we don't know what Evan might be driving, can we find out?" I asked. "I don't want to leave Kathy and the kids alone, so I'll stay inside and keep an eye on the car for any sign of movement."

"You got it, Tom. This could be the break we've been waiting for. I'll see what I can do from here."

"Thanks, Jerry," I said as I was hanging up. I almost dropped the phone when I felt a warm breath on the back of my neck after scented hair lightly brushed my ear.

"What's going on?" Kathy whispered.

"Be very quiet and don't move," I said as I found the door handle in the dark and closed it as quietly as I could. Reaching for her hand, I turned and pulled her close so I could speak softly into her ear without waking the kids. "It may be nothing, but there's a car parked across the street. Jerry is sending a patrol car over to investigate. Do any of your neighbors on that side of the street own an older model Toyota Camry?"

"Nobody around here does. Most of them drive American cars."

"I'm going to watch the car until the police show up. Whatever you do, don't make any noise or turn on any lights," I said. "Go close the kids' doors so we won't wake them up. We don't want them turning on lights either."

Kathy returned from the hallway and slowly eased the door shut again. "The kids are still sound asleep," she said with a whisper while standing behind me.

I had assumed a squatting position at the windowsill while holding the bottom slat of the blind up with the binoculars. Other than the occasional glow when the car's occupant took another drag on his or her cigarette, I still couldn't discern any facial features or determine hair length.

It wasn't long before a patrol car emerged from a side street with its headlights on. The Toyota's engine sputtered to life, raced down the street, and turned left at the next intersection with the cruiser in hot pursuit, lights flashing. There didn't appear to be a license plate on the back of the Camry. I muttered to myself, *I told Jerry to make sure he didn't get a rookie to respond.*

Turning to the door, Kathy said, "Since we're up anyway. I'll make a pot of coffee."

I had just settled down with a mug of fresh steaming brew and another stack of Kathy's homemade chocolate chip cookies when my cell phone rang. "They lost the car," Jerry announced.

"Well, tell the kid who was on duty to turn out his headlights well before he rounds the corner next time," I said out of frustration.

"I'm sorry, Tom. That was the only cruiser available in your area of the city."

"I didn't mean to take it out on you. I know you've put in a lot of hours here and you're probably as disappointed as I am that we lost him. Don't worry, we'll get him next time. I'll talk to you and Janyce later today. Try to get some sleep."

"They couldn't keep up with him and don't know where he went," I said to Kathy.

"Jerry and Janyce have been alternating their cars with yours in the driveway to make him think there was someone here when I was alone with the kids," Kathy said. "They also attached a recorder to my home phone. Jerry said Evan has been using a burner cell phone that can't be traced."

"Well, we'll figure something out to catch him, so don't worry about it," I said as I sipped the coffee to wash down another toll house cookie.

"I feel much safer now that you're here, Tom. I don't know how I can ever thank you enough."

"You could begin by cutting back on the baking before I start packing on the pounds. It's been quite a while since I've enjoyed home cooking."

40

I must have been more tired than I thought. The sun was beaming in the window when I opened my eyes. Karen and Kevin were almost sitting on top of the television watching cartoons with the volume slightly muted. Kathy walked by in the hallway but was back in a flash to set a steaming hot coffee mug on a cork-lined ceramic coaster next to me atop the small table the recliner shared with the adjacent sofa.

Upon noticing I finally had both eyes open at the same time, the K kids jumped up into my lap. Karen was busy giving me a flurry of kisses while Kevin was satisfied giving me a big hug around the neck before he sat on my knee, never averting his eyes from the TV screen. After hearing Kathy's suggestion that they give me enough space to breathe, Karen sheepishly slid down to my other knee.

Kathy inquired as to what I would like for breakfast. I told her that anything that's easy would be fine, including dry cereal. She noted that I must be starving after not eating much on the flight the day before, but I assured her that anything handy would go well with the coffee. It certainly would perk me up enough for when Jerry and Janyce showed up to create an action plan. Kathy insisted I dump the kids back on the floor and join her for a bit of peace and quiet in the kitchen. With that accomplished, I spied the remote on couch. I turned the volume back up a few notches before leaving the room, much to the kids' delight.

Kathy proceeded to throw a pat of butter in the frying pan to melt while she whisked a couple of eggs with a dash of milk. She must have anticipated how hungry I really was when she added the contents of a small bowl from the fridge to the mix that had chopped onions, mushrooms, and peppers. Then she threw the composite blend into the greased pan. Turning down the heat, she covered the omelet to be. Kathy then joined me at the kitchen table with a cup of coffee of her own.

"I must say I didn't realize that I'm famished. That smells absolutely delicious," I said as I started to salivate.

"After you flew across a whole ocean to get here, it's the least I could do. As much as I try not to show it in front of the kids, you don't know how worried I've been. Thank you so much for coming, Tom," she said as she popped up out of her chair. "Woops, I almost forgot to put in the toast."

"Relax, we'll get this whole mess straightened out so you can get back to your normal routine."

"I don't know how much more of this I can take. The kids have classmates dropping off their homework with instructions from their teachers, but I don't know if they will be getting too far behind with their class work. Quite frankly, I'm having trouble trying to figure out how to help them with this modern approach to math," she said. "It just doesn't make any sense to me."

Kathy rose to flip the omelet and then slide it on a plate for me. "More coffee?"

"That was great, but I'll nurse this one a while thanks," I said with my hand over the top of the cup. "I know what you mean though. I went through the same thing with the modern math stuff with my kids too. You'd think they would have given up on that approach by now and revert back to the tried and true rote methods."

"Would you like some homemade strawberry jam for your toast?"

"No, thank you. This is terrific, Kathy," I said as I proceeded to fill my face, savoring the fluffy masterpiece she had just created.

"I just remembered that I'm starting to run low on a few staples," Kathy said. "That was the last of the eggs. I'll be glad when this is over with so things will get back to normal. Then I can return to work before they end up replacing me."

"Don't worry about that. Why don't you make a list of what you need and have the grocery store send it over so you don't have to go out? Does Guido's Fresh Marketplace on South Street deliver?"

"I don't think so, but Harry's Supermarket over on Elm Street does. Good idea, thanks."

"Who could that be at the back door?" Kathy said as she jumped out of her chair when the doorbell rang once.

"Kathy…," I said in frustration when she threw the Louverdrape in front of the patio door open.

She was greeted by the smiling faces of Janyce and Jerry, but I said, "Don't ever answer the door by yourself. Please let me do it just to be on the safe side."

"I'm sorry, I just wasn't thinking. This whole mess has me so confused that I can't function anymore. I'll try to be more careful from now on. I promise," Kathy said as she crossed her heart.

"How did you two get behind the house without us seeing you?" I asked.

"I thought we had discussed this in detail, Tom," Janyce said. "We parked on the next street and walked through the neighbor's backyard to get here so it would appear that Kathy might be alone. We only had to hop one fence to get away from a scrappy little dog with a mean disposition. Next time I'll have some Kibbles and Bits in my pocket to throw to him."

"Good thinking. Maybe that will encourage Evan to try something stupid when he feels confident enough that we won't be waiting for him," I said.

"You know where the closet is. Hang up your coats and have a seat at the table. I'll pour you each a cup of coffee. What's in the box?" Kathy asked.

"That's a silly question, Dunkin' Donuts of course. What else do you think a pair of cops would bring?" Jerry said.

"I was running low on supplies, and Tom suggested having a few groceries delivered. Is there anything special I should add to the list for you?" Kathy asked.

"You must be kidding about that too. I don't have the willpower that Janyce has, and you've been feeding us too well. Please don't get any more sweets. I have no resistance. When this is all over, I'm going to have to get back to the gym and start working out again," Jerry said.

"Okay, I'll call dibs on that chocolate frosted raised doughnut. I don't understand why Kathy insisted on putting them on a plate when they'll be gone in seconds," I said. "We could just eat them out of the box."

"You men are all the same. If we didn't put out napkins, you'd be using your sleeves," Janyce said with a grin.

"Then what would we do with our sleeves, pray tell," replied Jerry, chiming in. "Might as well cut them off then."

"Hey, cut that bickering out. There's a reason we're meeting here. That's to figure out how to protect Kathy and the kids so they can get their lives back to normal," I said.

"All right, did we find out anything when the cruiser was chasing that car last night?" Janyce asked.

"They never got a look at the driver. There was no license plate on the back, but they were sure it was an older model black Toyota Camry. It was hard to tell at night, but it appeared shiny enough in spots to have been repainted recently. They lost track of it when they turned on Route 7 North," Jerry said. "They gave up on finding it after checking the few side roads in the area."

"Do we know if Evan has a car registered in his name?" I asked.

"Heck no, he even had his driver's license suspended, and it was never reinstated," Janyce said.

"I suppose we don't know if he has any friends in the area that would lend him a car," I said.

"The few friends he has who are not in prison live out of state. I think he lost track of all his old army buddies long ago. They probably gave up on him when he started taking up serious drinking again," Kathy volunteered.

"I can check recent stolen car reports in the area for a Toyota Camry," Jerry said.

"Okay, my car is parked a couple of streets east of here. You two can pick it up and park it at my apartment. I will stay here with Kathy and the kids while you see what else you can find out about Evan. Maybe his parole officer might know something we don't," I said.

Janyce and Jerry stood to leave. Jerry shook my hand and said, "It's great to see you again, partner. We'll keep you posted if we learn anything new."

"Be careful. Don't be a hero, cuz," Janyce said as she gave me a big hug and a peck on the cheek.

41

"Good morning, Tom. I don't know what you baked, but it looks and smells delicious," Kathy said.

"Hi, Kathy, I hope I didn't wake you. I just threw a French apple pie together. I figured that the kids might like something different for a change."

"How did you make the crust? I didn't think I had enough of the right ingredients. I know I don't have any shortening."

"It's called stirred pastry from my grandmother's recipe book. For an eight-inch, two-crust pie you need to blend two cups of flour with a half cup of oil, a teaspoon of salt, and one-fourth cup of whole milk with a fork. For a ten-inch pie, you just double the amounts."

"What did you use for a rolling pin? I don't have one."

"I pressed it out between waxed paper with a wine bottle. If you add a handful of raisins to the pie shell, it helps to soak up the apple juice as it cooks."

"What did you use to make the frosting?"

"It's one cup of powdered sugar mixed with a tablespoon or two of milk. I decorated the top with walnuts, raisins, and the maraschino cherries I found in the back of the refrigerator."

"It certainly is colorful. I'm sure it will be a hit with the kids. You didn't have to go through all that trouble, but thank you," Kathy said as she almost gave me a kiss on the lips, but I turned my head.

"It was no problem. I was getting a little cabin fever after not going out for the last week," I said.

"Maybe I read you wrong. We've been getting along so well and the kids are thrilled you're here to play games and read them stories at night. I thought you and I were getting closer too. Perhaps that's because I was so afraid of being alone before you showed up. I have felt so safe since you've been around. Is there someone else who is special in your life?"

"To tell you the truth, I don't really know where I stand. I'd been on my own since my divorce a dozen years ago. That is until a few months ago when I ended up with a partner who's fourteen years my junior. I saved her life, and she saved mine. In the field we have to depend on each other. Somehow we became involved along the way. I kept telling her that I'm too old for her and she should find someone closer to her own age, especially if she wants to have children someday."

"It sounds to me as though she already has made up her mind that you're the right one for her."

"She doesn't seem to listen to me when I say she can do a lot better with someone else. Her life expectancy is at least fifty years while I'll only be around for another thirty, if I'm lucky. That's crazy. I already failed as a father and husband. As a cop, I just wasn't available when my family needed me. She's got her whole life ahead of her."

"How do you feel about her?"

"She's a wonderful woman and has everything to offer that any man could want in a mate. I miss her a lot. I'm just not sure that I want another wife in my line of work. Then there's the race thing."

"What race is she? Don't tell me you have a problem with her because of her race?"

"No, of course I don't. It's her father. He doesn't want her to even date or work with white guys. He thinks if he has grandchildren, they shouldn't have to put up with being misfits who are rejected by both the whites and the blacks."

"That sounds like it's his problem, and it shouldn't bother you if it doesn't bother her."

"Can we please end this discussion? I've had this argument in my head too many times without reaching a conclusion. Every time I try to figure out how to let her down gently without hurting her, I end up with another migraine."

"I'm sorry. I didn't mean to pry, but it sounds like you have to make up your mind."

"I have, but she won't take no for an answer. She's wonderful, and I care for her a lot. I know that she would be short changed with me as a partner in life and she could do a lot better. That and I'm convinced I don't want to get married again."

"I don't know how I can help. So we'll just change the subject. I hear the kids going at it again. Let me quiet them down, and I'll come back and fix breakfast," Kathy said.

Kevin's eyes bugged out when he saw the decorated pie cooling on a wire rack next to the stove. "Wow, is that for breakfast, Uncle Tom?"

"No, it isn't. That's for dessert after dinner if you kids behave yourselves and do everything your mother asks you to do today," I said.

"Aw, sometimes you're no fun at all," Kevin said with a pouting expression written on his face.

"Kevin, that's no way to talk to Uncle Tom after he worked hard to make you something special," Kathy said as she entered the kitchen followed by Karen. "Tell him you're sorry and you'll be on your best behavior today."

Karen suppressed a giggle because as usual her brother was in trouble again.

Kevin looked down at the floor and after a long pause said, "I'm sorry, Uncle Tom. I'm just tired of being cooped up inside and want to go to school with my friends."

"I know it's not easy, Kev. Hopefully it won't be much longer before things to get back to normal," I said as I mussed his hair.

Kevin's mini-tantrum was interrupted when I was summoned by my cell phone. It was Janyce. To find a little quiet and privacy, I walked into the guest room as we talked. I tried my best to keep Kathy informed without raising her hopes too much or having her worry about details that don't pan out.

When I returned to the kitchen, the kids were seated at the table having breakfast. I signaled for Kathy to follow me into the living room where I informed her that there was no news. It was as if Evan had been mysteriously swallowed up and disappeared somewhere. No one had seen or heard from him. Jerry and Janyce would be stopping off at the house this evening.

42

We had just finished dinner when the doorbell rang with a single chime, so I knew it wasn't the front door, which would ring with a double tone. I said it must be Janyce but told Kathy to sit still while I made sure. Turning off the lights, I opened the blinds enough for Janyce to enter through the patio door in the back of the house. To prevent our activities from being monitored on the outside, I closed the blind again before turning on the light again.

Janyce had greeted us and the kids before joining us at the table for a cup of coffee. I may have imagined it, but I thought I heard the sound of a car door closing. Grabbing the binoculars, I went into the guest room to take a look. Sure enough, a dark-colored sedan was parked up the street. I dialed Jerry who picked up almost immediately.

"Jerry, where are you?" I asked.

"I'm a few streets away, why?"

"Janyce is here. There's a car across the street again. It may be Evan. I'm going out the back door and circle around the block with her car. If you come down Chestnut Street and block his exit, I'll approach it from the back side in about five minutes. Keep your cell phone on, and I'll let you know when I'm ready to turn the corner."

"Jerry, here I come. I'm coming up behind him."

"Gotcha covered, Tom. I'll block this end of the street."

In an effort to get away again, Evan raced down the street, shooting wildly out the window in Jerry's direction before smacking into the side of Jerry's unmarked car.

I pulled up behind him to prevent any chance of escape. Evan was still stunned when I raced to pull him out of the car. "Jerry, I got him, are you okay?" I said.

"I'm all right, Tom, although I can't say as much for my car. That idiot plowed into me broadside. Is it still called a T-Bone when he bounced off me after we collided?"

"I've got the cuffs on him. Let's get him into the back of Janyce's car and down to the station. Give Janyce a call first. Tell her that none of Evan's shots hit us or her car. You can say it's all over for Kathy, and we'll be back in a little while. The good news is that we've got him for an armed assault on a police officer this time. That should add several years to his sentence."

"Hi, girls, how are you holding up?" I said as I entered the house later.

"Tom, I'm so glad you two weren't hurt," Kathy said as she ran to give me a hug.

"Well, Evan is back behind bars where he belongs. Are the kids okay?" I asked.

"I put them to bed after you left. I'm so relieved, but I still can't stop shaking. I don't know how I can ever thank you all," Kathy said.

"It was just a little old-fashioned teamwork. I'm happy it's over for you," I said.

"Jerry, I was worried about you too. I wish there was some way I could repay you and Janyce too for all the time and effort you put in on my behalf," Kathy said while giving Jerry a big hug, apparently not willing to let go easily.

"Do you need to go back to the station tonight, Tom?" Janyce asked.

"No, I completed a full deposition. According to the assistant district attorney, my testimony, and the paperwork Jerry will finish tomorrow will be sufficient for the trial. Once we determine that Jerry's car is safe enough to drive home tonight, you can drop me off at my apartment. Thank you both for all your help. I couldn't have done it all by myself."

"Tom, I don't know what to say. I've been barely making it from one paycheck to the next without child support. I wish I could pay you something. Thank you for giving me my life back. When will I see you again?" Kathy asked.

"I have to get in touch with Langley, but I'll try to stop and say good-bye to the kids tomorrow before I leave if I have time. Take care of yourself and try to relax. Evan is going to be put away for a long, long time."

"Jerry's car didn't seem to be damaged too much to drive home, even if he couldn't use the door on the driver's side to get in," Janyce said on the way to drop me off at home.

"Better the car than him," I said. "I'll have to give Joan a call to find out how she is doing on her own."

"Even though I didn't really spend much time getting to know her, from what you've told me, she sounds like a lovely woman. It's too bad you think she's too young for you," Janyce said.

"No, that's backward. I said that I'm too old for her. I just don't know what I'm going to do about her. I'm happy when we're together, but I know it just can't work out between us."

Because we've always been so close, at times it seems like Janyce is more like a sister to me than a cousin. It was hard to say good-bye to her after all she had done for me, especially not knowing when I would see her again. I just drew comfort in the knowledge that she was always there for me when I needed her.

Looking around, my apartment appeared barren, devoid of any personality. Maybe I should put up some pictures of my kids and friends I've had through the years. A few splashes of color and curtains or drapes wouldn't hurt either. It was odd I never noticed that before. Is that because I spent time with Kathy who had made her house a home for her and the kids, or was it Joan's positive influence on me?

If I didn't know whose apartment this was, would I call it naked, unfinished, or what? It certainly was what you'd envision when describing a typical bachelor pad. I guess nobody does live here. This was a place where I merely slept after long days at work chasing bad guys or locating missing persons. Most nights I only managed to keep my eyes open long enough to avoid bumping into a wall trying to find the bed. Then I would scramble out the door in the morning to arrive at an appointment in time without taking a moment to see what the "pad" looked like in the morning either.

Would it be different if Joan were part of my life on an ongoing basis? Apparently my work always came first. Was that out of necessity, or was it just that I didn't want to carve out enough time for my family? Was there a way I could have convinced the police captain I really needed to be at the kids' ball games or recitals instead of working a double shift because the department was shorthanded? I can't put the blame on my ex-wife for any of that. It was entirely my fault. I honestly don't know how I could have done anything differently, short of going into a new line of work.

I'm too tired to think about all of this now. I can't call Alex at Langley to find out how Peter and Monique Pickering are doing. It's too early to call Joan in Switzerland at this hour. What would I have to say to her anyway that she hasn't already heard? I'll just tell her that this case is wrapped up, and I'll probably be on my way back after I talk to or meet with Alex.

43

I had the first full night's rest in over a week, not requiring vigilance by sleeping in a semiconscious state while trying to discern if any of the normal house noises could be Evan trying to break in. I called Alex at Langley after brewing a half pot of coffee, which almost had me completely awake. Fortunately he was still there, trying to tie up loose ends with Rob so he could become fully dedicated to his Middle-East reassignment.

He said the Pickerings had returned to their house in the Berkshires since the doctors didn't think they could help Peter any more than the constant attention provided by Monica's ongoing tutorage. They felt that being back in familiar surroundings at home could offer Peter additional sensory stimulation. He had come a long way with Monica's devotion to his therapy, but was still somewhat vague about the details of the attack that put him into a coma.

Rob, Alma, and Joan were actively seeking the whereabouts of Li Yang and Imugi. Rob was coordinating efforts with the manufacturers in the United States to assure the components destined for shipment to North Korea were segregated by special internal part numbers from their standard inventory without their employees being aware of what was going on.

Alex agreed that I should go back to Switzerland to help find out if Li and Imugi were the only ones working for North Korea in Europe while we try to find these two Asians. I thanked Alex for his help with the Pickerings and wished him well in his new assignment.

I checked for flights to Zurich finding US Air 3958 had a cancellation connecting to Swiss Air in Boston if I could get to Albany, New York by 5:30 PM. The twelve-and-a-half-hour trip time wasn't that much worse than the eight hour direct flights from the NYC area. I found a 1:40 PM Greyhound bus could get me from Pittsfield, Massachusetts to the airport in an hour, so I repacked my suitcase and made reservations for a cab to get to the bus terminal. I would have to give Kathy and the kids a call later when I had a chance.

I called Joan's cell, but she must have been talking or had her phone turned off because it went right to voice mail. I left a message that I would be arriving on Swiss Air flight 53 tomorrow at 11:00 AM, her time, and asked if she could please pick me up at the Zurich Airport.

Knowing that the meals on the international flights were not any more filling than the ones on the domestic trips, I fixed a frozen Healthy Choice "Golden Roasted Turkey Breast" meal in the microwave oven. The gravy and stuffing weren't exciting, but the green beans were okay. The cherry blueberry dessert was too sweet for my taste, but as a whole, it had to be better than what Swiss Air had to offer on the overseas leg of the journey. At least my tummy felt full after and the meal would tide me over until the meager offering of airline food was available in-flight.

The Greyhound bus arrived on schedule at the Albany airport. With time to kill, I started reading a new mystery/romance novel entitled *Wispa* by an author named Tim Parker. Apparently it's about a couple who end up working for the CIA to find the foreign terrorists trying to poison Boston's water supply. I wondered if this writer was related to Robert B. Parker who wrote the *Spenser for Hire* and Jesse Stone series novels.

It only took an hour to get to Philadelphia. It almost seemed like once I was seated and buckled in, I was on the ground again and had to change planes. The connecting flight to Boston took a little over an hour. Then I had to wait for another two hours at Logan Airport to board Swiss Air 53. It always seemed to me that most of the crashes one hears about on the news involve an Airbus. Here I was taking two of them in a row. Not a comforting thought.

I must have been more tired than I had imagined. The next thing I knew, I was landing in Switzerland. If they did serve an in-flight meal, I'd slept through it. With two plane changes in the states, I was glad my carry-on was safely stored in the overhead bin. That will help get me through the customs line sooner than the passengers who had checked their luggage.

Once I made it to the ground transportation area, Joan was waving to me from the crowd, waiting behind the roped off area with Alma standing next to her. Joan rushed up to give me a big passionate kiss once I broke free from customs. Not knowing if Rob was aware that Joan and I were a couple, I glanced around the area looking for him.

"Did you miss me?" Joan asked anxiously with a big smile, looking positively adorable.

"Yes, of course I did," I said, knowing I meant it.

By then Alma had walked up with a grin because she was in on the secret between us. Alma gave me a hug and a buss on the lips, saying, "Welcome back."

We followed Alma out to her car. Pulling my bag behind me, Joan latched onto my other hand, swinging our arms like we were a couple of carefree school kids involved in our first crush.

After I loaded my bag into the trunk, Alma said, "Since you two have a lot to talk about, why don't I drive and you can sit in the back together?"

No sooner were we seated when Joan whispered in my ear, "Have you thought more about us being together on a long-term basis?"

"Don't you think this is something we should discuss in private later?" I said quietly.

"She won't hear us with all the noise from the city traffic," Joan said.

"Okay, but you may not like what I have to say. I haven't changed my mind. I think you'd be better off with someone else. I wasn't very good as a husband or as a father for my kids. I enjoy my work and know I can't stop in the middle of an investigation and punch out on the clock at 5:00 PM. It wouldn't be fair to you," I said.

"I knew you were going to say that again. I've been thinking about us too. I don't want anybody else if I can't have you. I happen to like what I do for work too. That means I can't start and stop what I'm doing on a set schedule either. Look into my eyes and tell me again if you really missed me," Joan said.

"I'd be lying if I told you I didn't," I said.

"Do you love me?"

"I can't deny how I feel about you either, but I don't think I can make you happy enough to last a lifetime," I said.

"Let me be the judge of that. I've never really had feelings like this about anyone else. I know I've been much happier since you came into my life, and I don't want to give you up. You know they say, 'Half a loaf is better than none'? I only want you, even if it is for part of the time. I'm not letting you get away," Joan said.

"Joan, you wanted this assignment and the CIA has a strict policy about fraternization for good reason. This could jeopardize your whole career. I don't even know how much longer I'm going to be in Europe. I don't think we should get involved any more that we already have," I said.

"We already are involved, and there's no way my feelings for you are going to change. Alma won't tell anyone and we can be careful around Rob. As long as we don't have any PDAs, my position will be safe," Joan said.

"I'll bite, what's a PDA?" I asked.

"It stands for 'public display of affection' silly, now come here and kiss me before I attack you in front of Alma," she whispered hoarsely in my ear.

"Hey there, you two, if you don't stop distracting me with all that mumbling and fogging up the windows, I won't be able to drive. Do you want to stop somewhere for lunch on the way back, or do you want to get a room?" Alma said, grinning into the rear view mirror.

"I thought you'd never ask about lunch. I'm starving," I said.

We spotted a small Lithuanian family restaurant a few blocks down the street, which was great because I was famished. I probably should have backed off on the Lithuanian liquor the host kept refilling my glass with because I was really getting sleepy.

Returning to Alma's apartment, we had a message from Rob that he would drop by at ten in the morning to talk about what had transpired while I was away. I was going to lie down on the couch for a few minutes to rest, but it was pitch-black the next time I opened my eyes.

44

I was so tired I must have drifted off back to sleep, but at some point in time, I woke feeling pleasantly warm. It was then I discovered Joan had cuddled up on the sofa next to me. Since she appeared to be on the verge of falling on the floor, I pulled her closer to me. She moaned and snuggled up even more yet so I gently woke her up and suggested we go to bed.

"I'm so glad you're back. I missed having you around and worried about your safety," she whispered softly in my ear on the way to the bedroom.

"Shhh…you'll wake up Alma," I said.

"I don't care. I want you so much I'm going to rip all your clothes off with my teeth," Joan said as she pulled me down on the bed with a mischievous gleam in her eye.

"Aren't you worried that this might drive us both nuts? Wanting each other so much with nothing definite for a long-term basis?'

"There is no tomorrow, love, only today. There will be nothing later, just this moment in time. We'll live in the here and now and not waste any of it. If we are together later today or tomorrow, we can enjoy being with each other again and make the most of that too. We can try to be quiet, but I need to be close to you in every way possible tonight," she said, wrapping herself around me.

Later in the morning, Joan went into the bathroom to shower while I wandered toward the kitchen in search of the delightful coffee aroma that wafted through the air of the apartment like a delicious cloud.

"Well, good morning, if it isn't Rip van Winkle. At least you don't look as tired as you did yesterday," Alma said, filling a mug of coffee for me.

"Hi, Alma, thank you, I think. It's good to be back."

"I'm surprised you finished your assignment so soon. I take it that all went well and your work is done in the colonies," she said.

"We caught a lucky break. The dummy we were after came to us, and we nabbed him when he was being stupid. It was almost as if he wanted to return to prison. Now his ex-wife and kids can get on with their lives instead of living in constant fear."

"I suspect you are being too modest, but whatever works for you. Joan has been moping around while you were gone, merely going through the motions of getting through each day. She was thrilled to get your message yesterday that you were on the flight to Zurich."

"I kept telling her that she could do better than me, and I wasn't geared to a long-term relationship, but she says she's okay with that," I said.

"Well, I've seen the way you two interact and can't say I know of another couple with a better fit. If she's pleased with this arrangement, you should stop worrying and let yourself have fun too. If things change one way or another down the road, you can address it then. Just don't take a chance of missing out on all the happiness you obviously share now," Alma said just before Joan entered the kitchen, looking well scrubbed with a towel turbaned around her head.

"And what were you two talking about when I came in the room?" Joan asked.

"Nothing much, I told Tom that you seemed surprised yesterday to hear that he was coming back so soon. Coffee?" Alma asked.

"Yes, please. I'd love a cup," Joan said.

I described in detail to Joan and Alma what had transpired in the states, including the fact that Peter had made sufficient progress to finally return home to the Berkshires with Monique.

"That's fantastic. Will someone be looking after them in case there is another North Korean agent lurking about in New England with mal-intent?" Joan asked.

"Jerry and Janyce will be checking on them along with periodic patrols by the Westmorland gendarmes," I said as Rob pulled up to the curb.

"Good morning and congratulations on your promotion, boss," I said as I held the door open and extended a hand to greet him.

"Well, technically, since Alex was the one who hired you on as a consultant, I'll have to find out if you report to me now," Rob said.

"Okay, until you verify I'm still on the case, we'll leave it at *gutten morgen* then," I clarified.

"Maybe I could figure that out better with a cup of coffee in my hand. Hi, ladies, nice to see you and welcome back, Tom," Rob said.

"This coffee should be strong enough to clear out the cobwebs," Alma said with a deep smile, handing Rob a steaming mug.

Blowing on the coffee to cool it, Rob took a slow sip and said, "Ahh, thank you…that's just what I needed to pick me up. I've been running on vapors lately."

"Have we had any feedback on the whereabouts of Li Yang and Imugi?" I asked.

"There's been no word on possible locations for Imugi, but Interpol called me while I was en route this morning. They said that Li Yang used a debit card in Basel at Steinenschanze Stadthotel. They don't know if he's still there, but he checked into room 157 yesterday," Ron said.

"Well, we'd better be on our way before we lose track of him again. We probably should take two cars. Joan and I can try to get there first to cover the back of the hotel before you go in," I said.

I'll drive while you sip your coffee so you won't spill it all over yourself," Alma said, grinning.

No sooner were we underway on the road to Basel when Joan said, "I wonder how long those two have been working together?"

"Why? They seem to make a pretty good team," I said.

"It could be my imagination, but they appear to be more than just partners," Joan said.

"Just because we had to take vows of responsibility for each other doesn't mean that they did too. Maybe they haven't had occasion to save each other's lives yet."

"Now that you mention it, that's never happened with any other partner I've ever had in the field before. Do you suppose it's Kismet?" Joan asked.

"Don't tell me you are getting superstitious on me now," I said.

"I never believed in fate before, but have we just been lucky together so far? I feel fortunate to have ended up with you as a partner," Joan said with a far-off look in her eyes.

Not knowing how to respond to that based on our earlier conversations, I just kept driving. If I were looking for a lifetime partner, I could never find someone as wonderful, caring and thoughtful as she is. Unfortunately every fiber of my being keeps screaming stop—it doesn't make sense. I'd just end up spoiling everything for her and that would make me very unhappy.

We rode the rest of the trip in silence, lost in our own thoughts. It wasn't long before we arrived at the Steinenschanze Stadthotel. I drove around behind the building, and Joan called Rob on his cell phone. "Hi, Rob, we're in place in the back. Where are you?"

"Just pulling up to the curb in front, what does it look like back there?" Rob said.

"There's only one exit next to the fire escape. Tom said he'd go around to the front to make certain we don't miss Li Yang if he gets past you. I'll link Tom's phone on as part of a conference call and watch the back while you two go in," Joan said.

"Okay, we'll go in as soon as we grab our vests from the trunk," Rob said.

"Roger that," Joan said.

"We're at the end of the hallway on the second floor. We'll be entering the room in about two minutes," Rob said.

The sound of Rob breaking in the door to the room was followed by silence. "All clear on this end. You can come up. Li Yang isn't going anywhere. He was garroted. I'm told that was one of Imugi's trademark methods of assassination for those associates failing to meet his expectations," Rob said.

Joan and I arrived at the room about the same time. "There is no sign of a struggle, so Imugi was pretty fast. The body is still warm, we must have just missed him," Rob said.

"It looks as though he went through Li's things before he left. I understand he usually is careful about not leaving incriminating evidence behind that might come back and bite him in the butt. We could dust for fingerprints to see if anyone else was involved and check for other clues anyway," Alma said, looking around the room for anything that might have been missed.

"Without additional information, we don't know if anyone else was involved. We'll have to revert to the original plan on following up on the Three P customer list to see if we can find out where else Peter went on his business trip before he went missing," Joan said.

"We'd better get out of here before we end up wasting the day filling out reports for the Swiss Police. You go out the back way and we'll leave by the front door. We'll meet you at Alma's apartment," Rob said.

45

"Well, it's been three weeks since we found Li Yang's body. We're still no closer to determining where Peter was attacked and if there were others involved that we don't know about. Our plan to foil the North Korean weapons plot to use digital components from commercial American products for weapons manufacture could be in jeopardy if it's discovered prematurely. We've checked the rest of Peter's customer list and his charge cards without finding additional information that could have been useful to us," I said to Joan and Alma over coffee.

"I just received an e-mail from Rob. He's on the way here with some kind of big news that he wanted to share in person," Alma said after reviewing the message on the screen of her laptop.

"Hopefully it's good news because this waiting to see if the Trojan Horse Plan will work is painful because it's not under our control," Joan said.

"I think that's Rob's car pulling up in front now," I said.

"Rob seems to have a little extra spring in his step, so maybe it is good news," Alma said.

Rob burst through the door and said enthusiastically, "Well, our plan with North Korea's new supplier chains seems to be working. We're hearing reports from most of the countries that have bought weapons from North Korea in the past that their guns and rockets are exploding prematurely after very little use! Since their customers are not happy with them, that should drive all the third-world countries away from any reliance on Kim Jong-un as an arms supplier."

"That's great to hear. Mission accomplished. I wonder what they'll do with all those retrofit factories they set up?" I said.

"Wait there's more. Rumor has it that Imugi was summoned home to North Korea, but he's had a conspicuous absence since then. Nobody has seen him. We heard from our inside agents that he was assassinated for screwing up the whole operation that his Fearless Leader was counting on for a revenue stream," Rob said.

"So Imugi didn't live long enough to become a full-fledged dragon after all. Since we managed to shut down North Korea's program to become a significant weapons dealer, I guess that means my work is finished here," I said.

"How does that impact my assignment, Rob?" Joan asked.

"My understanding is that they want you to return to Langley for a briefing on another high-priority potential field assignment. I don't know what it is, but I understand it might be dangerous and you are under no pressure to accept it. It probably would involve a promotion for you. They only want to present the opportunity to you for consideration," Rob said.

"Of course I'll go and listen to what they have to say, but what will Alma do without a partner for backup in the meantime?" Joan asked.

"Don't worry about it. Alma and I have always been able to complete our assignments as a team. We can manage by working together again for the time being. Since we don't know if and when our paths will cross again, we can go out and celebrate tonight, my treat. I happen to know a little authentic Bavarian Swiss restaurant called Bierhalle Kropf. It's not far from here and the food is terrific," Rob said.

When we arrived, the hostess didn't speak a word of English but managed to communicate with sign language to seat us in a relatively "quiet" corner amidst all the festivities. Somehow she knew enough to give us the menus printed in English. Between the four of us, we managed to order a little bit of everything and pass it around to share family style. None of us were disappointed with the selections.

Rob had to go home after, so he was elected to be the designated driver for the evening. Unfortunately it appeared that Alma was getting a little sloshed with too much wine. She almost cried about how much she was going to miss the two of us. In between she dropped several hints about Joan and I being such a great *couple*. When she remembered she should not mention that in front of Rob, she tried to correct herself and say she meant *team* the first time. The next time she said *couple*, she corrected herself to say that we were great *partners*. Rob's raised eyebrow suggested he appeared to be getting the point that the two of us were much closer than he'd originally suspected.

The bottom line was that the food and camaraderie we shared all evening was wonderful. We had become so close working together, it seemed as if we had known these two forever. We managed to get Alma back to her apartment safely. Joan got her changed and tucked into bed while I made coffee for Rob before he had to drive home.

With Alma half out of it, Joan and I retired to the bedroom for a session of uninhibited lovemaking where we didn't need to worry about making noise for a change. Then we slowed the pace down to make it last as long as possible. At the end of our marathon, we just held each other for a very long time, because we didn't want to let go. Before we went to sleep, Joan shed a tear, kissed me tenderly, smiled and said, "Thank you for everything and being you."

I had no idea how I could or if I should reply. Coming down from cloud nine and thinking about that, it seemed to take forever before I could drift off to sleep.

46

Joan and I had an early breakfast. Then we cleaned the kitchen before we made plane reservations to return to the states. We decided to fly to Newark together and go our separate ways from there.

Alma arose about noon, looking absolutely terrible, complaining about a hangover headache. She didn't mention anything about what she had blurted out in front of Rob, so we didn't bring it up.

We offered to make lunch for Alma, but she said she positively couldn't handle anything more than coffee, which she nursed while Joan and I went to pack for our return flight to the states.

Alma insisted she was feeling better when we bundled her into the back seat of her car and put our luggage in the trunk. She said she would return the rental we'd been using with Rob later since it was leased in his name anyway.

Joan snuggled up to me as I drove to the airport. When we arrived at *departures*, Alma was sound asleep. I removed our bags and placed them on the curb while Joan woke her up. Once Alma appeared to be fully conscious with her eyes wide open, she said, "I'm going to miss the two of you so much. Love you both."

"Hey, we'll be in touch. Who knows, I might be back here for my next assignment," Joan said as she gave Alma a big hug.

Alma surprised me by giving me a long, passionate kiss on the lips, backed up, pointed her index finger at me, and said, "You listen to me, Tom Powers, you'd better take good care of her or you'll have to answer to me."

"Thanks for putting up with us, Alma. Who knows, maybe I'll come back someday on another assignment, but we can keep in touch regardless," I said, handing her the keys.

Alma waved as she drove away. I guess I felt as sad as Joan looked because we may not see her or Rob again.

Once we were seated on the plane and headed down the runway, Joan held my arm with both hands as she looked up to me and said, "I know we've hashed all of this out, but I still feel as though something was lost in the translation. There just seems to be a major piece of the puzzle that's missing. I understand your reasons for not wanting to be involved in a long-term relationship again. I also agreed to do it your way, yet I still have a real problem with it."

"Joan, the only regret I have with our relationship is that it has caused you grief. That is exactly what I wanted to avoid. It's for the best that we make a clean break of it so you can get started on a life of your own. Then you can be happy with someone your own age you can relate to who shares the same values," I said.

"That's the whole point, Tom. I was never truly happy with anyone until I found you. The guys I'd met who were my age were too superficial and immature. I know you don't want any more kids, but I've kind of decided that the only reason I was considering it at all was to appease my dad," she said as the tears started to flow freely down her cheeks.

"Don't punish yourself this way and prolong the agony. I couldn't put you through what my ex-wife had to endure with me. She never knew when or if I was coming home. When I promised I would be somewhere for her and the kids, I was always in the middle of something I couldn't break away from."

"If I'm at Langley and you're in Massachusetts, we could meet halfway on weekends or at least get together once a month." she said as she tried her best to muster a smile while drying those beautiful eyes which were becoming red from crying.

"That would only postpone the inevitable and keep you from finding true happiness with the person who is totally right for you. I know I can't be that someone for you. I care for you too much to hurt you that way."

"Okay, okay, you can't blame me for trying. I'll put on my big-girl face and behave myself. I need to ask you one question though."

"All right, what's the question?" I asked.

"How are we going to be responsible for each other if we are that far apart?" she asked, looking up at me with an adorable crooked grin and a sniffle.

"I thought we agreed that the debts canceled each other out when you saved my life in Switzerland."

"I think the only one that will be happy with this arrangement is my dad so he doesn't have to take a chance on having grandkids with polka dots," she said as the *fasten seat belt* light went out, and she turned to give me the longest French kiss.